REVOLUTION

THE LAZARUS ALLIANCE, BOOK 4

BLAZE WARD

KNOTTED ROAD PRESS

Revolution
The Lazarus Alliance: Book Four
Blaze Ward
Copyright © 2021 Blaze Ward
All rights reserved
Published by Knotted Road Press
www.KnottedRoadPress.com

ISBN: 978-1-64470-201-7

Cover art:

ID 76082241 © Luca Oleastri | Dreamstime.com

Cover and interior design copyright © 2021 Knotted Road Press

Reviews
It's true. Reviews help. Even a short one, such as, "Loved it!" So please consider reviewing this book (and all of the ones you've read) on your favorite retailer site.

Never miss a release!
If you'd like to be notified of new releases, sign up for my newsletter.

http://www.blazeward.com/newsletter/

Buy More!
Did you know that you can buy directly from my website?

https://www.blazeward.com/shop/

ALSO BY BLAZE WARD

The Lazarus Alliance

Escape

Return

Rebellion

Revolution

The Jessica Keller Chronicles

Auberon

Queen of the Pirates

Last of the Immortals

Goddess of War

Flight of the Blackbird

The Red Admiral

St. Legier

Winterhome

Petron

CS-405

Queen Anne's Revenge

Packmule

Persephone

Additional Alexandria Station Stories

Siren

Two Bottles of Wine with a War God

ONE

LAZARUS

LOOKING IN THE MIRROR, Lazarus felt like he still hadn't stopped running in nearly a year. Not since that first battle with Westphalia that almost saw him and *Ajax* destroyed, and had instead launched him on perhaps the greatest adventure in several centuries.

Now, he'd fought a second battle. Redeemed himself, at least in his own mind. Shattered two GunWalls, crippled a Heavy Starcruiser, and recaptured the planetary system at 6357 Wei Xiu, commonly known in the fleet as "Vilga's Stand" after the legendary Almirante Vilga who inflicted one of the first great defeats on Westphalia, Earth's government, when the Rio Alliance sought to break free.

They'd spent a week in-system since the most recent battle. The one he'd won.

Ajax was almost as good as new, with all the construction equipment on hand for the station Westphalia had been building, and the extra crew of engineers and gunners he'd brought with him.

He could head home right now. Return to the capital world of Brasilia and be a hero. As it was, they would probably take a look at what he was about to do and Court Martial him. Maybe even strip him of his pension for what was coming next.

Even if it was the right course of action.

Lazarus studied that stranger in his cabin mirror's reflection, wondering about the new lines in his face and the gray hairs starting to come in among the orangish hair on the sides. He knew he'd lost weight, but a year ago he could have probably stood to drop a few kilos. Not ten.

The man staring back was an older version of that crazy kid who'd joined the military and been turned into a special forces killer, before they decided to turn him into a naval officer. Lean and drawn, but it was the stress now, not a late growth spurt back when he was seventeen. Working too many hours and not eating as much as he probably should, in spite of Khyaa'sha trying to stuff more food down him every chance she got.

Lazarus checked the time and decided he'd spent long enough hiding in his quarters. He needed to step out into that corridor and turn himself back into the severe commanding officer of the Rio Alliance's most deadly warship, the experimental Light Starcruiser *Ajax*.

He checked his uniform one last time, took a deep breath, wondering if Thadrakho was going to need to take the pants in yet again, and walked to the main hatch from his cabin.

Outside, the rest of the ship waited patiently for him. It would. He was in command, and needed to start acting like it again. Less time repairing things and more time planning for an unknown future.

He turned aft and stepped onto the slidewalk, gliding like a man ice skating on the repulsor fields. Two marines stood as a sort of guard when he reached the flight deck. Gunners with small arms certifications that had gotten pressed into duty for today, just so everything looked more official.

Both saluted smartly, then one opened the hatch.

Lazarus stepped into the main flight lounge and found everyone already waiting for him, but that was again by design.

Addison Wolcott and Eha Dunham stood in a corner, coiled tails twined and holding hands. Their heads were together as if they had been whispering quietly. Both looked up now and the scales around their eyes flared a little in embarrassment, like he'd caught them necking or something.

He might have, knowing those two.

Lazarus grinned at them and counted noses around him.

Engineering Chief Garcia was already aboard the station, working furiously to get everything on line before the fleeing Westphalian fleet could somehow return. Xiuying Bălan, the ex-marine he'd picked up on Yisan, had swapped billets with Lucas Lam and was over with Garcia.

Lam was at attention by the hatch to the bay itself, but he was the odd newcomer with this group and he knew it.

All the original crew of *Shiva Zephyr Glaive* was present today.

Lazarus smiled at Aileen as she stood up and grinned. Rio Navy Commander rank looked good on her. Wybert of Capantzina stood next to her, his breastplate painted in the same tan. He had even left his powerspear somewhere else, wonder of wonders.

Kuei Akeley, Lt. Commander and *Ajax*'s pilot for now, looked like she'd rather be going with Addison, but Addison had gotten overruled by Lazarus. He still needed her here, at least until he could find someone who was as good a pilot as she was. If there was anyone.

Ereshkiki Nisab and Thadrakho had come forward from Engineering, but they had left Lt. Commander H'Brige Slani in charge, and even Lazarus, formerly an engineering nerd turned commander, was impressed with that Atomarsk woman's chops.

Even the two Crawlers, Cormac and Lenox, were here, but *Ajax* could fly on autopilot for a time if it had to.

Everyone wanted to send Addison and Remahle off in style. Addison would be replacing Eha back at Brasilia as Ambassador to the Rio Alliance, while Remahle had finally gotten his wish to go off and have some adventures of his own, after Lazarus had taken Aileen with him both times before this.

Lazarus paused and looked around. He was still missing someone.

Oluchi Pryce had been left behind on Brasilia.

Grace stepped into view from wherever she had been practicing being invisible and Lazarus felt a weight vanish off his shoulders. He and she still needed to have a conversation about things, but that would be next on his list after getting Addison sent off.

Right after committing mutiny.

Maybe at that point he could consider doing something personal. After all, it had only taken Addison and Eha a decade before admitting they had feelings for each other.

Lazarus studied the man as Addison slithered close, still holding hands with Eha. Addison was wearing a maroon vest today, rather than the tan ones that had marked him as a temporary Rio Alliance officer.

"You could remain in tan," Lazarus reminded him, yet again.

Addison just grinned.

"One of your admirals might take offense," he said. "Worse, they might decide to keep me in uniform. If I am not on the deck of *Ajax*, I am a civilian. They need to remember that."

He paused, glancing over at Eha with a mournful smile.

"Plus, I am her representative now, so this is a diplomatic mission, as well."

Eha leaned close and put her weight on the man's shoulder.

Lazarus had never been a particularly emotional person. He was the first to admit that, but he had to fight back tears right now. Odd, but appropriate.

The entire situation had started *out of hand*, and then gotten worse.

It would only get *more worse* from here.

He was going to miss this man. After Aileen, perhaps his best friend in the universe, and about to walk into the lion's den with Daniel and ask God for another miracle.

But then, so were they all.

Lazarus of Bethany, who had once been Francisco Luiz *Pancho* Oliveira, *Capitão De Mar E Guerra*, was about to go cause a ruckus, in direct contravention of all of the orders he had received.

But then, maybe in addition to being reborn from death, he needed to occasionally tilt at windmills.

Grace happened to be standing beyond Eha such that he could just see her past the Churquen woman.

Would she make a good *Sancho Panza* for what was coming?

Lazarus nodded to himself, unsure but certain that it was time. He turned to Remahle, the Kr'mari cargo hand that had been Aileen's assistant for years. A man who had never really gone on adventures, because he tended to go along the familiar path.

Not a leader, but a solid follower, and the Navy and the galaxy needed people like that as well.

"You ready for an adventure?" he asked the man.

"You bet," Remahle laughed. "Gonna find me a tall building with a fast elevator so I can fly."

Lazarus laughed with the rest of them. Kr'mari looked like a four foot tall glider squirrel, wearing a kind of jumpsuit that went between the legs with a hole for his tail, and over the shoulders, but with both sides open for his membranes. Like the others, normally tan, representing impressment into the fleet, but he had reverted to being a civilian with Addison, so he wore blue today.

Lazarus turned back to Addison.

"I will miss you, my friend," he said simply.

Addison nodded and shook his hand solemnly before turning to kiss Eha one last time, and then slithering out the hatch Lucas opened.

Remahle joined him and everyone moved to the window to watch the two of them board the cargo shuttle, the pincke that Lazarus had borrowed from his support squadron.

"All hands to duty stations," Lazarus said in a conversational voice, turning to head for the exit. "We should give them a proper sendoff."

Everyone had their place in the coming revolution.

Hopefully, they would all survive it.

TWO

EHA

EHA FOUND IT ALMOST BIZARRE, being on the bridge of *Ajax* without Addison here, but that was going to be her fate for a time. They were swapping stations in life, him as the Ambassador to the Humans, and her returning to Innruld Space as spymaster, so that the long-sought revolution could actually begin.

She had spent her entire life in preparation for overthrowing the Innruld, those so-called masters of the galaxy that had kept all the other species in chains. At least until now.

She had understood that *Ajax* and Lazarus were dangerous before, but until the battle for Vilga's Stand, she had not truly appreciated what they could do. The Innruld built Security Barcs and Pyramids to dominate space.

The Humans built warships. Eha Dunham understood the difference now.

Nothing they would encounter could stand before Lazarus and this ship.

She looked around the bridge from what had been Addison's station, a cone he had installed to one side of

Lazarus's seat, where she would sit at the Director's left. Except that Humans didn't have Directors. They had Captains of Sea and War. Lazarus of Bethany.

Perhaps it was for the best that she was here and not Addison. She had tasted her lover's rage a few times since they had become fugitives. Lazarus would simply overthrow the power of the Innruld.

Addison Wolcott might yet be the kind of man who would hunt them all down individually, just to end the species. But then, he had spent more than a decade smuggling various narcotics for her. The kinds that caused the Innruld to develop lethargy and ennui sufficient that they stopped breeding.

Eventually, they would have died out on their own.

Addison in possession of *Ajax* wouldn't have had to wait generations to succeed.

"Stand by for redshift," her lover's voice came over the communications line.

She watched on the big screen at the front of the room as the vessel nosed carefully around to a point in the darkness. The Humans called it a cargo shuttle. A pincke. And yet it was more than a third of the size of *Shiva Zephyr Glaive*, Addison's ship. But the warship Eha found herself on was nearly a mile long. Slender like a Churquen, with three fins aft unlike any snake she knew.

Deadly. There was no other word for it.

Rio Alliance Light Starcruiser *Ajax* was about to become the most lethal thing in Innruld Space.

As Addison's ship vanished in a burst of crimson, Eha considered that perhaps *Ajax* was going to become only the second most dangerous thing in Innruld Space.

Eha still had a debt she owed.

Time to go collect.

THREE

ADDISON

BLUESHIFT. That tremendous flash of light indicating the arrival of a ship leaping through a hole in the universe. Addison was still getting used to the concept, because he had spent decades using Innruld technology to get around.

Open a tunnel and navigate politely around. Slower, certainly. More certain, though, as you could twist around objects in your way, instead of jumping as far as you could go in a straight line, then turning to go around stars and other heavy things that dimpled space-time.

Four jumps had landed him in Brasilia. The heart of the Rio Alliance. The allies he still hoped that he could recruit to help Eha and the Species Underground to break the Innruld.

Hopefully they wouldn't be so angry at *Ajax* and Eha slipping away that they took it out on him, but that was an outcome Addison had prepared himself for. He had even considered attempting to talk Remahle out of accompanying him, as they might both be thrown in a Human prison shortly, but Addison agreed with Aileen that he deserved a chance to see some of the sights that he had missed.

Again, hopefully not the inside of a prison cell.

According to Human flight rules, he was in the Inbound Lane now. Nearly at rest, relative to everyone else and more or less under the guns of one or more of those defensive fortifications that Humans used to keep other Humans from attacking.

He took a deep breath and looked over at Remahle.

"Let's get stupid, Addison," his sidekick/copilot said brightly.

Like maybe the Kr'mari had a clue how dangerous everything had just gotten.

Addison keyed the line and picked up a piece of paper with the number printed on it.

"Brasilia Inbound Operations, this is vessel 15698723 in the Inbound Lane, holding for flight instructions," he read off the sheet Lazarus had prepared for him.

Low profile, as only a military vessel would have the records to know that this pincke originally came off of the Protector/Leader vessel sent to Vilga's Stand with Lazarus. To anyone else, he was just a cargo shuttle making a run.

"15698723,what are your movement orders?" a man's voice came back relatively quickly.

Again, a military thing. He even recognized the terminology.

"Returning to Brasilia with updates," he said. Again, everything ambiguous on an open radio line that anyone could listen to.

Longer pause this time. Addison wondered if the Human was talking to a warship on another band, vectoring them down on top of him quickly, in case there was trouble.

"15698723, come to these coordinates and stand by for rendezvous," the controller finally said.

Addison checked the file attached and triangulated against where he was now.

Short slither sideways. Good enough.

"Understood, Flight Control," he said. "Stand by for transit."

Addison programmed the coordinates and took another deep breath. Every step was one closer to the swamp, and Churquen didn't swim worth a damn.

Still, he was here, and had a mission he needed to fulfill.

Blueshift.

All the scanners lit up immediately when he emerged. Addison looked down and realized that there were several warships in close proximity. Almost surrounding him.

"15698723, this is *Recife*, on your port flank," a woman announced in a friendly-enough voice. "Who's piloting today?"

"Addison Wolcott," he replied with a grin he felt all the way down to his keelscales.

Like the shuttle's hull number, it wouldn't mean anything to most people, but it was certain to get someone's attention. He didn't say Commander Wolcott, because he was done being in uniform. This was a civilian mission.

Another voice came on the line now. Male. Sounded older.

"Confirm the pilot's name again, 15698723?" he asked.

"Addison Wolcott."

There. Deal with it.

"Stand by, Commander," the man said. "We are opening the starboard landing bay for you. Go ahead and dock when ready."

Huh.

Someone knew who he was, alright. But this was *Recife*. Almirante da Silva was probably still in command. Someone Lazarus had nice things to say about. Eha as well.

He scanned the monstrous whale on his left and watched a light come on about two-thirds of the way back as a garage door opened slowly.

Addison maneuvered adroitly, bringing the bow around on gyros instead of thrusters and sidling up with a slow slither, like he was stalking a galumph in the high grass.

He entered the giant's maw and settled on landing gear and magnets, feeling the ship close up behind him and begin to pressurize.

He had arrived.

Now to see what the Humans had to say.

FOUR
OLUCHI

OLUCHI HAD SPENT a fortnight in a gilded cage.

Oh certainly, a pretty one. Still in the palace of government, well south of Greenbriar, on a massive reservation of trees and wilderness artfully sculpted to look natural. Excellent food. Reasonable hours. They had even started letting him have better wine with meals.

But it was still a cage. He was still being watched everywhere he went, with at least two minders any time he stepped outside his personal suite after someone had managed to suborn things back when he had only had one. His days now were spent negotiating excruciatingly-precise minutiae of contracts that would hopefully go into trade agreements with the former-Innruld Space, once Lazarus and Eha were done.

But Oluchi had come to appreciate that he'd been dreaming far too small originally. Back on Yisan, the folks he was representing here didn't spend all their days on such deals. They had people for that.

Oluchi wanted to have people.

Still, this was better than living in a cell. Or returning to the life he'd been trying to escape on Yisan, a gigolo on the far side of pretty and starting to run out of options.

If these deals began to bear fruit, he would be probably end up rich.

For now, he stood on the balcony and looked out over the late afternoon sun as everything turned slowly crimson overhead and the shadows in the extended garden stretched.

Balconies were another upgrade. His previous suite had windows that could not be opened from the inside.

It wasn't like he had anywhere to run to at this point. Oluchi was the one left behind when the important people had left the system, and everybody was hoping that they would come back for him one of these days.

A knock at the door to his suite, back inside, preceded the door opening and closing.

"Oluchi?" she called.

Anya. The spy who had been originally assigned to seduce him for information. It had turned into something of a two-way street. A most pleasant one, too.

"Here," he called.

Anya joined him a moment later. He was leaned over the rail while standing, so she did the same. The woman had proven to be enough of an exhibitionist that he occasionally wondered if they might spend an interesting evening out here at some point. But the sun was still up, and there were people moving around below in the garden.

Oluchi glanced over at her, appreciating that it was a nicely gilded cage, at that. She was cute but not blessed with the sort of beauty that would stop traffic, although her bottom might if she wore tighter pants. Hair lightened to a soft brunette contrasted nicely with copper skin and hazel eyes that didn't miss much.

The brain was almost frightening, if you didn't like them smarter than you. Maybe even if you did.

She stared back with a knowing grin on her face, so she was in on some secret that had as yet not been sent his way.

Oluchi considered whether he'd have to tickle it out of her later. Or whether she'd tell him now and he'd do it anyway.

As she had observed on more than one occasion, *the sacrifices we make for good government.*

"Did you have dinner plans?" she asked vaguely, eyes bright and lips pursed.

"I appear to be at looser ends than normal," Oluchi retorted. "Unless some daring knight comes along to rescue me from this dreary tower."

"Funny you should mention that," she laughed. "You should dress up tonight."

He had noted that she wore a nicer, gauzy gown in arboreal patterns over a black bodysuit today. Just thin enough that most men would be trying to steal a peek until they realized that everything was covered. And maybe still anyway.

"Do tell," he turned and leaned his hip on the wrought iron railing now, taking her all in. She'd even gotten so daring as to wear makeup tonight, which was uncommon bordering on rare for Anya. But she didn't need it.

"Erlyn Teixeira has permission to escort you off premises for a nice dinner in Greenbriar," Anya said. "I've been assigned as your minder for the evening."

"Have you now?" he grinned.

She grinned back, also turning inward.

"Indeed," Anya agreed. "Reservations are in an hour, so you just have time to get changed. Wear the gray tonight."

The Gray. The Rio Alliance High Council had decided to treat him like an Ambassador after Eha left, and that had involved a tailor arriving and taking all his measurements. Upon moving into the new suite, there was a whole closet of outfits in varying degrees of formality waiting for him.

Including a gray suit that flashed maroon, paisley patterns when the light hit it just right. Top of the line work, too. Oluchi had considered how he might steal it later.

"Anything for you," he smiled and began to move.

Oluchi had been expecting a cloud to pass over her face. The line was rather automatic coming out of his mouth, and every once in a while he meandered into emotional minefields with the woman. At least he had come to understand that very few of said mines were his fault.

He was just the fool charged with disarming them. If it took years or even decades, he could think of far worse ways to spend his time.

But her face stayed cheerful. And a professional poker player like him could tell with almost every person he encountered.

Oluchi stopped, turned, and pulled her close before she could react, pressing Anya against his chest.

"Too bad they waited so late to invite me," he said, kissing her.

Her arms came up around him and he felt her heart rate. It was hammering far harder than it should have been, but she returned the kiss with passion that had been missing at the beginning of their little assignation three weeks ago.

Back when it might have just been a job for the both of them. Hopefully, good things would come of it, although if forced to choose then he'd steal her away and leave the gray suit behind.

Given the opportunity.

"Are you okay?" he asked as they stopped to breathe.

"Mostly," Anya said. "Things are in motion and I'm not privy to them. Erlyn is getting very serious in ways she was not before."

"Let us hope that is good news, then," he forced a smile and kissed her again.

Kissing her didn't get old. She seemed to agree.

Eventually, she stepped back and pushed him.

"You need to get dressed," she ordered in a mock-severe voice. "We have a double date tonight."

"Do we now?" he grinned, starting to pull off layers and toss them onto the bed. "Business *before* pleasure?"

"Always," Anya agreed readily.

Oluchi wondered what had changed.

FIVE

ADDISON

ADDISON WATCHED two lines of sailors emerge from the far end of the lock and march forward, coming to rest next to a line of red carpeting that two engineers were carefully rolling out.

It did not look like today was going to be an informal sort of thing.

Everyone outside came to rest as he finished powering things down.

"Should I be scared?" Remahle asked, fidgeting in the copilot seat.

"No more than me," Addison replied. "But you know as much as I do."

"Oh, goody," was all Remahle had to say in a dry voice.

But Addison agreed there, as well. At least none of the sailors he saw were armed, near as he could tell, so they weren't planning on arresting him.

What the hell they were doing wasn't something he was ready to guess at.

Instead, he slithered aft to the lock, checking once to make sure that the interior pressure was good. Humans preferred an atmospheric density and gravity field that was frighteningly high. They must have come from a hell world originally.

But he had also gotten used to it, having left *Ajax* at the settings Lazarus preferred.

The hatch opened now and Addison heard music playing. The day was just going to keep getting weirder, wasn't it? He didn't recognize the tune, then he did.

Crap, they're playing the Rio Alliance Navy's theme song? What the hell?

The opening of the hatch had galvanized the sailors, who had snapped to rigid attention.

Addison turned to Remahle with a grim smile.

"Just play along for now," he said. "Don't ask any stupid questions or offer your opinion on anything unless I ask for it, okay?"

"Hey, would I do that?" Remahle asked, slightly hurt.

Addison gave him a stern look.

"Oh, right," Remahle concluded. "Gotcha."

Addison took a deep breath and slithered into view. It was interesting that none of the sailors reacted badly, but then, this had been the vessel where Eha had originally landed, so they had all presumably seen a Churquen in the scales before.

Two men stood perpendicular to the line of sailors at the far end, where the rug ended, so Addison headed that direction, grateful for a warm carpet on his keel instead of cold metal.

Human males. One was a captain, from the tab on the collar. The older one was an Almirante. An Admiral.

Addison was doubly happy that he was playing a civilian today. Those men might have objected strenuously to him wearing the uniform they had served for decades. He had merely been the best suited to take over when Lazarus needed to be elsewhere.

Still, he was a Director. He understood the pomp that they had rolled out today. Checking that Remahle stayed close, he came to a stop about a body length from the two men and nodded politely.

"Admiral. Captain. Thank you for the welcome," he said.

The admiral was studying him closely. Shrewd eyes, even if they didn't slit properly.

"Commander Addison Wolcott?" he asked in a louder than necessary voice. He gestured to his comrade.

"At one time, sir," Addison replied carefully. "I have returned now in place of Ambassador Dunham, who has been called away. As such, I also return to civilian life. This is Remahle Mebarsu, from my crew."

Both men surprised the hell out of Addison by snapping to attention now and saluting, joined a moment later by THE ENTIRE ROOM.

Addison returned it, at something of a loss.

"Rodrigo da Silva," the older man introduced himself. "Captain Paulo Quispe, commander of *Recife*, although I suppose you would call him a Director. Admiral Santos has briefed me on what you did at 9087 Geminorum IV. Thank you. How did it go at Vilga's Stand?"

Addison studied the two. Glanced back at the rest.

"*Ajax* proved out her builder's expectations with great success, Admiral," Addison said carefully. Deliberately.

Lazarus had said good things about da Silva. H'Brige Slani and most of the rest had come from this very vessel, and proven themselves exceptional as well.

"Casualties?" Quispe asked in a quieter voice. Nervous. Those would have been the people he had been responsible for.

"Two sailors with broken limbs from a container that

hadn't been strapped down properly," Addison grinned. "One nearly drilled a hole all the way through his leg with a power tool on the station."

"Station?" da Silva asked, a little surprised.

"*Ajax* routed the Westphalian forces, Admiral," Addison replied, unsure he should be having this conversation in public, but what the hell? He had all the data Lazarus had sent along. "The station was about half done and surrendered rather than being annihilated. The Westphalian fleet extracted the construction crew and departed, badly mauled if I understand Lazarus's terminology."

Just because, Addison turned to the two lines of troops.

"Your cohorts saved my tail," he called loudly. "And stomped hard on theirs."

The men and women over there hooted and cheered.

Addison nodded to an apprehensive Remahle and turned back to the officers.

"I have the complete logs for you from Lazarus," he said.

"He did not accompany you?" da Silva asked in a leading voice.

"He did not," Addison replied, just as carefully.

The Admiral turned to another officer in the longer line.

"Commander, stand everyone down and announce an extra ration of rum with dinner," da Silva called. "Once we sort it all out, sounds like we'll also have a formal celebration."

More cheers from the sailors. But they were all volunteers, and their friends had impressed the hell out of Addison.

The two senior officers turned to depart and beckoned Addison to follow.

He did, making sure that Remahle stayed close.

Now the hard part would begin.

SIX

LAZARUS

LAZARUS STUDIED the wall of gases and stars displayed on the big screen.

"Phraettis Nebula," he mused aloud. "Is it strange to anyone else that it feels like I'm coming home?"

Kuei rotated her head over a shoulder and flipped both ears vertical with a grin.

"You were born here," she observed with far more sarcasm than a simple pilot should have, were this still a military vessel. "There's always that."

They had left most of the new crew at Vilga's Stand, save for one of the gun teams and a handful of engineers to provide enough bodies to be on shift around the clock. *Ajax* was still designed to fly with a minimal crew.

"True," Lazarus agreed. "And I still don't know how I managed to find a hole through there to Innruld Space. Part of the reason I needed you piloting, Kuei. You know the far side of the shield far better than anybody else."

She harrumphed in his general direction and turned back to her screens. Lazarus turned to Eha, seated close.

"How about you?" he asked, noting the way her scales

moved. Smooth and relaxed, but also nervous with suppressed excitement.

"Coming home?" she replied. "Yes. But for different reasons. It's not really a home for me or my kind. But if we're successful, it might become one for our children."

"Did you tell Addison before he left?" Lazarus lowered his voice to a whisper.

The guilty way her scales flared around her eyes and jaw as she looked at him in shock told Lazarus what he needed to know. The sound of her tail thwapping against the nest inside her coil was just confirmation.

Eha stared at him in horror for several seconds.

"How did you know?" she finally sputtered in quiet shock.

"I've been a sailor for a number of years, Eha," he said carefully, trying not to smile at her. "Women sending their mate off on long voyages often do that. Plus, you've gotten more serious. More focused on a distant future than just tomorrow."

"So you couldn't tell?"

"I wouldn't even know what to look for," Lazarus said.

"Oh," she said, finally calming some. "Don't tell anyone?"

"Absolutely," he nodded.

But he understood. She was measuring things in generations now. A side effect of however it was that Churquen got pregnant. That was what had suggested her condition to him in the first place. There weren't places he could look such things up, at least not until he got to Innruld Space and maybe stole or bought a medical book or three.

Lazarus nodded and looked back up at the bridge. Like Kuei, Wybert was at his station. Cormac had an extra camera up and extended backwards, so Lazarus pointed at him and then put a finger to his lips for silence.

It took the NavCrawler a moment. Probably had to look up Human physical idioms in the computer, then Cormac nodded his camera.

People forgot how much the Crawlers were programmed to notice, mostly because they ignored most of it and weren't gossips. But Cormac was over a century old at this point. He'd seen a few things in his time.

Lazarus was still getting used to a computer sophisticated enough to be considered sentient. Or occasionally tell dirty jokes. Human cultures didn't use them. Westphalia didn't trust such slaves, and the Rio Alliance didn't want to deal with the ethical quandaries that intelligent machines presented.

"Pilot, you know the route I took to get in there originally," Lazarus said louder now. "And the route we took coming out and going to Yisan."

Kuei looked back again, her ears far more laconic now. Almost horizontal. As if daring him to question her awesomeness.

"So, with access to *Ajax*'s star charts, and your experience, is there a better way through?" he asked. "Akeley's Passage, if you will?"

He watched her eyes light up, but Lazarus also understood that she was almost as nerdy as him, just into geography and piloting instead of power systems and naval architecture.

"You in a hurry?" she asked.

"According to Aileen, we'll run out of food in about a year," Lazarus teased back. "Think you can find us something prior to that?"

"Just you watch me, mister," she laughed.

Lazarus enjoyed hearing her laugh. They'd all been too serious lately. Hazards of the job, he supposed, coupled with the mission they were on now. There was a war coming, but it wasn't here today.

In fact…

"Kuei, you have the bridge," he announced, standing. "Everyone else stand down to whatever until your next duty rotation."

"Where are you going?" Eha asked as he turned and walked away.

"Kitchen," Lazarus laughed. "Khyaa'sha keeps trying to get me to eat more. Maybe it was time I listened to her."

SEVEN

OLUCHI

DOUBLE DATE. On paper, it sounded utterly droll and harmless. Oluchi Pryce was not the least bit fooled.

The limousine that had arrived for him and Anya was already occupied. Alliance block Human Councilor Erlyn Teixeira was there, dressed to the nines in a nice gown. Oluchi was introduce to the other woman with no name besides Manon. He thought it was a French name, but he wasn't sure.

The new woman was apparently an artist in just about every medium one could try, from the range of things that came up in general conversation on the flight to the restaurant.

Oluchi found it terribly interesting that he was the only male in the vehicle. Especially as Teixeira had apparently placed a bet earlier with Anya that Oluchi would attempt to seduce the older woman.

Possibly bisexual then, or at least open minded. Flexible about such things, in an era when not everyone was. And Manon was a most interesting person to chat with, dressed in a suit similar to his, but elegant black and simple. Refined.

It didn't make her look the least bit masculine, but certainly caught the eye. Oluchi supposed that to be the entire point.

They landed on a roof, disembarked, and rode the elevator down a few levels to one of those steak house joints that take up a whole floor and wrap the view all directions, depending on one's mood and need.

The sun was setting, so they watched the last of the color drain while sipping a good house red and nibbling on an anti-pasti plate.

Oluchi noted that the three closest tables had all been left empty, in what was otherwise a relatively crowded restaurant. He put that down to the Councilor's pull with the staff. She must use this as a stage to impress folks relatively frequently. Or talk business.

Oluchi smiled and considered how much the woman reminded him of Fernanda Flores, back on Yisan. Roald Cavalcanti was nothing like Eduardo Martìnez, but probably held about the same power ratio in their relationship.

And Oluchi had played a great deal of poker with Eduardo over the last few years, frequently for mind-bending stakes.

Oluchi smiled now at Teixeira. *Jacks or better to open?*

She seemed to feel the same energy, because she shifted forward in such a way that the general conversation at the table died like a knife had chopped it short.

"This is not generally known," the woman began, taking a sip of her wine and studying him across the small table.

They had ended up facing each other, but the other two really were just decorative tonight, weren't they?

He nodded.

"A vessel arrived in system a few hours ago," Teixeira continued, her voice much quieter now. "It rendezvoused with the warship *Recife*. The pilot of said vessel was apparently Addison Wolcott."

"Interesting," Oluchi offered noncommittally.

"Quite," the woman said. "Since it wasn't *Ajax* but a small transport. I think they call them pinks?"

"Pincke," Oluchi corrected her pronunciation. "A short-range cargo transport like the one Lazarus and Eha brought to Yisan, the first time. Is there panic?"

"Panic?" she asked, deflected. "No. No panic. Apparently the battle went well and the Westphalian forces were utterly routed."

"But?" Oluchi asked.

"Eha Dunham did not accompany Wolcott," Teixeira said without implying anything. "What might that suggest to you, Pryce?"

Oluchi smiled and called. They were early in the game, with only one card apiece showing.

"Perhaps Lazarus still finds himself lacking trust," he offered, just to get the obvious out of the way.

"Then why send Wolcott at all?" she countered.

"They still wish to maintain a thread of conversation with the one power in the vicinity that might be helpful to their cause," Oluchi guessed aloud.

"Might?"

"Has the High Council decided to supply Lazarus and friends with sufficient force to go challenge the Innruld's claim to dominance?" Oluchi decided to play a little rough now. Not much. Just showing the blade rather than actually using it on anyone.

Wouldn't want these nice clothes to get bloody now, would we?

"They have not, as yet," Teixeira said, glancing at both of the other women to remind them of state secrets. "That conversation is ongoing."

"And yet, the whole point of the Rio Alliance was to create a multi-species polity where all life forms were welcome and protected, wasn't it?"

Teixeira stirred uncomfortably.

"Some of my fellow Councilors express concerns," she offered as a polite way of suggesting that they were acting like Westphalians.

"Just so," Oluchi leaned back and sipped the wine. For a house blend, it was pretty good. "Did Eha empower Addison to act in her stead as Ambassador?"

Oluchi liked the way her eyes flared for just the slightest moment.

"And if she did?"

"Then he'll take over all these negotiations," he replied with just a hint of predatory grin. "I will become his assistant in that. Meanwhile, he and I can negotiate other trade pacts dealing with Yisan."

There. That is how you properly use a knife, madam.

He smiled as the implications of Churquen/Yisan trade that bypassed the Rio Alliance entirely manifested itself in her eyes. The amount of money to be made. The political ramifications if a whole block of aliens found the Rio Alliance an untrustworthy trade partner.

Oluchi smiled.

"Is Captain Oliveira that good?" Teixeira asked. "Or the others? You people seem to keep piling up accidents in such a way that you always come out ahead."

Oluchi nodded.

"Lazarus is that intelligent," he offered simply. "Eha and Addison as well. Plus, they are all utterly ruthless in ways that I don't think any of you have given them credit for yet, Madam Teixeira. Eha has been a spymaster for more than a decade. Addison smuggled things designed to cripple the Innruld as a species. Lazarus built *Ajax*. They are not people to be trifled with. Perhaps your fellow Councilors have spent too much time wrapped up in the ennui of politics ere now and forgotten what the outer world is like?"

She nodded, deep in thought.

"There are those people who suggest you should be isolated from Wolcott," she replied.

"If you wish to make enemies of the Species Underground, I can think of no better way, no faster way, to achieve your goals," Oluchi kept the smile but let her hear the blade in his voice. "The clock was reset by *Ajax* returning, not turned off. You will need to make your decisions and do it soon."

"Or?"

"You asked what it meant that Eha hadn't returned with Addison, Erlyn," he said, going so far as to use her first name now. But he wanted to make this a little personal.

"Yes?"

"To me, it suggests that *Ajax* kept sailing outward," Oluchi smiled. "That even as we speak, Lazarus and friends are going to Innruld Space to destroy those bastards."

"Can he win?" she pressed.

"How did the recent battle go?" Oluchi asked. "You used the word *routed* earlier."

"Two GunWalls and a Heavy Starcruiser," she said quietly, nodding to him that this was still a state secret to keep. "The admiral's report I read suggested that *shattered* might also be a good verb to use. I was not expecting that *Ajax* was such a dangerous vessel, Pryce. What has Oliveira built?"

"Vengeance, Madam Teixeira."

EIGHT

H'BRIGE

H'BRIGE SLANI WAS USED to being the odd person out. Atomarsk were the second largest species in the Rio Alliance, by raw numbers, but tended to stay on their own worlds much more than Humans did. As a result, she encountered few in naval service. There were none besides her on *Ajax* now, with the handful from *Recife* staying back at Vilga's Stand to help finish the station.

However, she was used to being around Humans primarily. Her boss on this ship was a Qooph. A sentient being built like two disks each about four and a half feet tall, and each a handspan wide, a wheel with an inner rim that made him thirty inches wide, give or take. With six eyes and six mouths on that inner rim, and spindly arms that came out of his axle, ending in six-finger claws.

Three of those eyes seemed to be studying her with humor, if she had learned enough body language. She had become his primary assistant, since too much of engineering was built with stairs instead of ramps and she was far more skilled than Thadrakho.

H'Brige could see ripping sections of stairways out and replacing them with ramps, when they finally had enough crew to spare.

"So now we come to the interesting part," Ereshkiki Nisab intoned in several voices.

Always the full name. Nobody had ever even used a nickname for the man. But if his own stories were true, Ereshkiki Nisab was at least fifteen centuries old at this point. He referred to other species as *ephemerals*.

The mind boggled.

"The interesting part?" H'Brige repeated.

He also had a tendency to make bold proclamations and then not continue unless prompted.

"You, Atomarsk Engineer Slani, are used to Rio technology," Ereshkiki Nisab said. "Far more knowledgeable than I, because Innruld uses radically different things almost everywhere."

She nodded, watching three eyes watch her. At least they were both standing still in the middle of the vast cavern known as Engineering, rather than rolling. Dealing with the being when he was rolling and those eyes kept tracking you made it really weird to watch.

"Where we are going, you will find things most interesting," Ereshkiki Nisab continued in a manner guaranteed to not arrive any time soon.

"How so?" H'Brige prompted.

"This is a secret you must now swear to keep," he said, pivoting somehow on his rolling feet until four eyes locked in on her.

The air felt colder, but she suspected that was just her. Atomarsk didn't have the strange, Biblical implications of running into a creature their holy book might have described as an angel visiting them.

At the same time, his grandfather might have visited Earth in that era and given rise to those very stories.

She nodded.

"My orders were to support Captain Oliveira," she said simply.

"Yes," he replied with what sounded like all six voices. "But this is Lazarus, not the Rio Captain Oliveira. There is a difference."

"How so?" she repeated, uncomfortable with where the conversation might be heading.

However, she also knew that they were technically in a state that might be construed by command as mutiny, depending on technicalities.

"We have left Rio Alliance service, Lieutenant Commander Slani," Ereshkiki Nisab commanded. "We are now pirates. You need to transform yourself appropriately."

She couldn't help the sarcasm in her face. Then wondered if Qooph could read an Atomarsk's body language. Where they were headed, her kind were merely legends.

"And?" she asked, talking now like a pirate rather than an officer from her tones.

The eyes and mouths all smiled, so she wondered if she had just passed some unknown test.

"Innruld technology is far behind Humans in almost all places," he said quieter, rather than booming such a statement across the entire bay for everyone to hear.

Including a few of her engineers from *Recife* who had volunteered to sail into the unknown with them.

"How far?" she asked, suddenly concerned.

She knew *Ajax* was more advanced than most ships, being brand new and experimental. How far ahead were Humans?

"Our life support systems are better than yours," Ereshkiki Nisab offered with a grin. "That's about it.

Weapons, shields, metallurgy. And we do not use star drives like you have."

"How do you FTL then?" H'Brige asked, feeling her tail separate out into individual blades behind her.

"Our trans-space drives open a hyperspatial tunnel that we sail through," Ereshkiki Nisab stated unequivocally.

"Sail?" She was aghast. *Like, slowly?*

"Sail," he confirmed. "We travel at a slow FTL rate between points, rather than blueshifting. It is still much faster than light, but much slower than *Ajax*. Or any other Human vessel."

Then the implications hit. Weapons. Shields. Hulls. Star drives. All in advance of Innruld tech.

"Pirates," she gasped as much as said.

The eyes blinked in a way that suggested something like a biped's nod.

"Any Human vessel would have an advantage on any Innruld vessel of matching tonnage," Ereshkiki Nisab said. "Thus the secrets of Innruld Space must be kept until the Species Underground can build or rebuild our own ships to Human standards. Overthrowing the Innruld as overlords is not enough, if any Human coming into our space can replace them."

"Oh," was about all she could say. Then a thought struck. "What about *Shiva Zephyr Glaive*?"

The cargorunner that the aliens had been flying when they first met Lazarus.

Again, Ereshkiki Nisab blinked happily.

"I look forward to having you and your staff aboard to finally get everything working correctly," he said. "Thadrakho is a good worker, but he is not an engineer by any stretch of the imagination."

"Can we upgrade the ship?" H'Brige asked. "Take some of our gear from *Ajax* over and replace your systems?"

"That is why we are having this conversation, Atomarsk Engineer Slani," Ereshkiki Nisab intoned in a much more serious harmony now. "It would not just be helpful. It becomes *necessary*."

She couldn't help but shiver all seven tail blades at the term.

7

NINE

ADDISON

ADDISON REALLY APPRECIATED that Eha and Lazarus had come through here first. The food he was served all contained things he was familiar with, none of which was poisonous. With the notable exception of the alcohol the two men were drinking over dinner. That much poison would kill him.

It just made most Humans a little silly.

Then again, they had to have originated on a hell world. Take this atmospheric pressure for example.

Rather than read the reports, or maybe in addition to it, Admiral da Silva had asked for a blow by blow account of the lead up and the battle. Addison had to remind himself that Humans were a violent species that enjoyed that sort of thing, so he kept in all the gory details.

"Is Kirov's Lance really that dangerous?" Quispe asked at one point, disbelief evident in his entire being.

"It is," Addison assured him. "I used it earlier myself on the pirates who I still believe were Westphalian sailors in a thin disguise. At short range, Wybert broke their ship into pieces. Here, we had managed surprise, plus Lazarus had enticed them into chasing after him, into the barrel arc of the weapon."

Both men made odd noises. Remahle shrugged when Addison glanced over. The few senior officers around the rest of the table made a point of eating without questions or commentary.

It was weird.

"So what is your mission now, Commander?" da Silva asked.

"Ambassador-Designate, please, Admiral," Addison responded. "I only took up the uniform because Lazarus needed me, and I have no interest in comparing myself to men and woman like you who wear it for a career."

The man nodded a little sideways as he chose his words.

"I've spoken with *Pancho*. Captain Oliveira whom you call Lazarus," da Silva said. "And spoken directly with Admiral Santos, who spent the most time around the man. We're honored to claim you as one of us, Wolcott. Not many people would have lived up to the standards we often fall short of ourselves. Shape and species don't matter. Plus, you are still up for a medal from the Admiralty Staff for what you did at 9087 Geminorum IV. I'm sure there will be another one for Vilga's Stand, as well."

Addison found that he could blush, but hopefully none of the Humans understood the flair of scales around his jaw and eyes to appreciate that.

He wasn't about to argue with potential allies, if they really wanted to reward him. That would help later when he asked for material help. They hadn't gotten there when it was Eha and Lazarus, but perhaps Vilga's Stand would help balance the scales?

Addison nodded. Took a breath and then a drink of the

tea that was about the only thing here other than water that he liked.

"There are two things in the short term, fellow sentients," he said in a heavier voice. "You need, we need, to get reinforcements to Vilga's Stand. The station is close to done now, but understaffed. And Lazarus left behind the three escorts to protect it, but that will not be enough if Westphalia comes back to try to reclaim it."

"And *Ajax* did not stay to protect the station?" Quispe asked.

Addison noted that da Silva remained silent, with perhaps a knowing smile on his face. But then, Lazarus knew this man, having served under him before, and had good things to say. Plus *Recife* had an excellent crew. Addison owed his life to those men and women, and the two officers in front of him responsible for them.

"It did not," Addison confirmed.

The details were in the report he was bringing, so this just made the secret known perhaps a few hours earlier than otherwise. But it needed to come out.

"Where did they go?" the Admiral leaned forward now to ask.

"Innruld Space," Addison replied simply.

"Why?"

"Lazarus and Eha both felt that this was perhaps as good a chance as they would get to return home and start their mission," Addison said. "Anything else risked *Ajax* being detained, either at Vilga's Stand or here at Brasilia."

"Start their mission?" da Silva asked. "What mission is that, Commander?"

Addison paused, understanding the immense weight of the words about to come out of his mouth.

He could feel a history book either start or end a chapter with this day. This meal.

These words.

"They've started the War of Liberation, Admiral da Silva," he said simply. "With *Ajax*, they are going to tear the Innruld down. Forever."

TEN

LAZARUS

HE'D BEEN WRONG. Looking at the Phraettis Nebula from the Human side hadn't been coming home.

Lazarus was now inside the nebula. Kuei hadn't yet found anything like Magellan's Passage, but she had a course that she could refine, given time. They were approaching the quiet ice giant out in the darkness where he had first parked a badly damaged *Ajax*, after that first battle.

Where he had put all his crewmates into the freezer until he could come back for them. And the ship. Where he had undocked a pincke and headed inward as he heard radio traffic that had sounded suspiciously like two smugglers handing off an illicit cargo as he got close.

Where he had first met Addison Wolcott and *Shiva Zephyr Glaive*.

The little treble clef cargorunner hung in orbit not far away as he watched on the main screen.

Now, he was finally home.

"Pilot, what is your status?" he asked Kuei unnecessarily.

Mostly just to get a rise out her, as she glanced back, ears pointed different directions to make her point.

"Anytime you're ready," she laughed. "We've been parked in a stable orbit for the last ten minutes. It won't degrade measurably for two years."

He laughed with her. They were both home.

"All hands, this is your captain," he announced into the intercom, hearing his voice boom back a moment later. "Stand by to begin transfer to *Shiva Zephyr Glaive* for operations. Engineering, whoever is in the final load will need to make sure everything is in full sleep mode."

"Understood, Captain," Ereshkiki Nisab responded harmoniously, so he presumed the Qooph would be traveling over with him.

Aileen and H'Brige Slani would be taking the original crew over. Aileen had already packed the pincke to the gills with gear. A few crew members and engineers would be crammed in for the short run over, but the rest would have to wait while Aileen and H'Brige got the life support systems back on line and the heat turned up.

Then they would start the process of turning her into a spy ship. Lazarus was just sad that he didn't have the space or power to dismantle one of the Star Spears and mount it over there. Wybert would have greatly enjoyed having something large to use on any pirates they encountered.

"Flight Deck to bridge, we're ready to depart as soon as Kuei gets her butt down here," Aileen announced.

Lazarus nodded to his pilot and watched her move. She stepped out of her station and leapt.

People mostly only saw that shuffling tripod that a Vaadwig was reduced to in crowded rooms with low ceilings. He had built the bridge in here with vaults because space was not at a premium.

So Kuei was able to use the full strength of those thighs and bound. Two long hops got her to the hatch, and then she was gone.

Lazarus wondered if he could keep up with her on the slidewalk, if she was on the deck just bouncing. Might have to race her sometime, because a Vaadwig could *move* when she wanted to.

He turned to Eha now, quietly seated nearby and taking it all in. She'd never been ship's crew, let alone navy, so she occasionally complained about being ornamental.

Eha Dunham was anything but.

"What are the chances that all stations have been notified?" he asked.

They'd had the conversation before, but no clean consensus had emerged.

"Zhoonarrim would have notified the rest in that sector," she confirmed. "Aceanx or Dormell. There is even a small chance that they sent a message to Gowook, my homeworld, but I think we're safe. If nothing else, they would bring us aboard the station to demand an accounting, not expecting a mob of armed Humans to pour out of the vessel."

"While Lucas might be looking forward to that, I can assure you that I'm not," he said sourly. "But hopefully you're right and we can pull a Trojan Horse on them if we have to."

She shuddered from her headscales all the way down to an unconscious thump inside her coil, but Lazarus wasn't surprised. Humans were violent. Much more dangerous than anybody in Innruld Space, the odd Kreeghal who wanted to Greco-Roman wrestle notwithstanding. A combat team of trained Humans probably factored high in a variety of nightmares for station authorities.

But he needed to do this quietly. If anything, Grace would do the damage, rather than Lucas Lam, because it would need to be *specific*, rather than generic violence.

Shiva Zephyr Glaive was going to be a Q-ship by the time they got to Gowook. A quiet, safe-looking little freighter, politely sailing along, until you uncovered an insane amount of violence, pirates suddenly running at you and taking over your ship when you thought you were about to take theirs.

"You should go get ready," Lazarus told Eha. "Aileen will have that pincke emptied out and back faster than you are expecting, since she doesn't need to do anything but have strong backs moving heavy boxes around."

Again the shudder. Humans could also lift over their heads two to five times the weight of what most other species could handle. The Yithadreph Loadmaster would be ruthless in exploiting that. He could speak from experience.

Still, Eha slithered away finally and left them.

"Wybert, you, too," Lazarus said. "Cormac and I can handle things from here."

Quickly, it was just him and the NavCrawler.

"*I could remain behind, Director,*" Cormac volunteered. "*Ajax would run much more smoothly if I was here to handle things.*"

"You're as much crew and family as the rest, Cormac," Lazarus said. "Remahle was right that he'd always been left behind when Aileen went off for adventures. You should not just be a footnote, either."

A camera came up and studied him.

"*What secondary plans should I thus be preparing for, Director?*" Cormac asked.

Lazarus laughed, but it was just the two of them. And the NavCrawler was the only one who had figured out that he was up to no good.

"Part of what we'll need for a successful rebellion will be ships, Cormac," he informed his quietest crew member. "I'm planning on having you roll right aboard one and steal it."

"*Steal one, Director?*"

"Would anybody suspect a NavCrawler, my friend?" Lazarus asked.

"*They would not,*" Cormac observed. "*It would be an utter violation of my primary programming to do such a thing.*"

Before Lazarus could reply, the little bot continued.

"*Good thing Addison Wolcott already reprogrammed me as a criminal.*"

Lazarus laughed.

Good thing, indeed.

ELEVEN

AILEEN

HOME.

Ajax was nice, but Aileen wanted to be home. *Shiva Zephyr Glaive*. Old, run-down, badly organized.

Also the ship she'd served on for the last several years.

She just wished she trusted things enough to open her faceplate and smell the weird funk of the ship. But they'd left it alone for too long. Too great a risk of something leaking out or in and poisoning things. At least they had atmospheric pressure, but she could tell that they were going to have to tweak things up for the Humans.

She'd be back to breathing swamp. And maybe trudging, if they turned the gravity up for Humans as well.

Aileen checked the readout on the inside of her helmet and walked forward. H'Brige could have done this better, but she didn't know what to look for, and they didn't have a Qooph rolling sphere. That left it up to her.

Into the side airlock where they had once—no twice—pulled Lazarus in during emergency situations.

Aileen chuckled at that. The glue her cargo harpoon used had left the faintest discoloration on the emergency suit

Lazarus had been wearing at Zhoonarrim. He still gave her crap about that to the point she'd considered having Thadrakho quietly, suddenly repaint the whole thing over and put the beer logo on his chest.

After all, the Innruld thought it was his family crest or something. Might as well screw with them as well.

Into the ship, she crossed the main cargo space, aghast that it was mostly empty, but they'd looted the place clean and put everything aboard *Ajax* that first time.

Engineering hadn't changed. A few dials were at the low end. Pressure and temperature were both dangerous, but easily fixed. And why she was fully suited up right now. Aileen stepped close to the controls and confirmed that there was enough water left in the tanks to crack for oxygen and dialed things up a notch. The engineers coming later behind her could fix everything once it was safe and they could do it without suits sealed up all the time.

Shiva Zephyr Glaive was old and worn, but had carried them to a lot of adventures. One more big one, maybe, and then the ship could go back to just running cargo. It would be a nice retirement, but she sure as hell wasn't about to buy all those maintenance headaches. Let the next sucker deal.

Aileen tweaked the gravity settings down significantly, once she checked the battery power. Might as well make this easy. Fuel tanks were still at three-quarters, so she brought another generator on line and let it start powering the heaters.

"Cargo One, this is Aileen," she said finally, after talking inside her head for the last five minutes.

"Go ahead," H'Brige replied.

She was in charge over there right now. Kuei was just flying for them.

"Everything seems solid over here," Aileen said. "Air is cold and light, but that's going to change over the next hour.

Gravity is coming down for cargo handling. How's the bridge holding?"

H'Brige and Ereshkiki Nisab had built themselves a semi-rigid tube to connect a Human pincke to a Innruld airlock so that cargo and people could be moved quickly. On this first trip, everyone was still in a suit, just in case, and bottled up tight. Next time, they'd get a little more relaxed.

Maybe.

"We're doing well here, Aileen," H'Brige replied.

Aileen grunted, mostly to herself.

Returning to the main cargo bay, she visualized everything and where it should go. No true cargo on this run. Instead, food for a bigger crew. Human equipment to maybe refit stuff over here to better tech. Gonna be a mess.

She couldn't help licking her lips in anticipation, though. Possibly the most complicated packing job she'd ever been handed, to fill *Shiva Zephyr Glaive* to the underside of the balcony with stuff. And she had Human backs and legs to do it.

At least all the damned storks in her life were going to be useful here.

Aileen reached into an outside pouch on her suit and pulled out a roll of colored tape. She paced the space off and put down a corner for the first box, along with an arrow indicating to the loading crew what they were supposed to be doing, because even Humans had no clue how to stack boxes correctly into the smallest cubic volume.

She surveyed it with a critical eye one last time. Good enough.

Inside pressure was coming up. Air had been about six degrees above freezing, but was warming up slowly. She'd be setting the heat regulator on her tub up a few extra degrees before she went to sleep, but **Oh My God** having her sleeping pool back was the single greatest thing she'd been looking forward to for a month.

Aileen looked down the maw of the airlock now and sighed quietly.

"Go ahead and open from your end, H'Brige," she said. "Box one and I've marked a spot on the deck over here."

The outer hatch began to beep as it opened, which was a good sign. It would only allow both doors open with sufficient pressure. And if something happened to the seal, it would slam both shut. Hopefully nobody would be in the way at the time.

H'Brige waved from the other end, and then stepped back. Atomarsk had no greater upper body strength or reach than a Yithadreph, all told. This was a Human job.

She knew all the Humans left on the crew, but they were faceless in suits today, with the exception of Lucas, who had added a gold stripe all the way around his helmet as an officer and security goon. It was apparently a Human military thing she didn't get, but she was back on her own deck now. Loadmaster of *Shiva Zephyr Glaive*, and they were going to be doing things *her way*.

She simply stepped to one side and gestured as the first Human came through, carrying a box too big for her to even lift. They'd take her old sled on the return trip, because the one from *Ajax* had been just a shade too wide to fit through the airlock over here.

The first figure moved quickly, setting the box down and aligning it with her lines. Looked male, so she guessed it was Afolayan, the one Battery Commander Wybert had left, with the rest of the gunner teams back at Vilga. He nodded at her and turned as the next person in line came through and tossed (*TOSSED!!!*) over a box.

Aileen smiled. Strong Human backs, working in a chain. All she had to do was keep them on line as the boxes and stuff came over and got stacked. And that pincke held a LOT of stuff. But that was why gravity was set so low in here that she had to be careful not to leap in the air, after so long at Human norms. One quarter of that would hold everything but the Humans could move fast.

Didn't even take that long, but folks had told her that smaller Human vessels frequently did it this way, so Aileen just stayed out of their way.

H'Brige and an engineering Petty Officer Four named Ishani Singh emerged as the gunners got everything emptied. With the pincke clear, they got to take a long break and eat, with the hatches sealed up.

Now, the fun part began. Both Navy women were in suits. Aileen would be hauling Ereshkiki Nisab's rolling suit back with her on the sled, but he wanted these two to spend some time familiarizing themselves with the systems over here. The physics and mechanics weren't significantly different.

Aileen escorted the women to engineering and showed off. A little. It was grungy and badly-lit compared to *Ajax*. Tiny, too, but you could almost put all of *Shiva Zephyr Glaive* in *Ajax*'s Engineering Bay, if you could move walls and generators out of the way.

"So, life support are these two," Aileen touched the systems currently putting out heat and air, and double-checked that nothing toxic had leaked.

She wasn't ready to open up and sniff just yet, but that was normal paranoia on a ship that had been cold for several months. Let the HVAC flush things and stir it all up. She probably had the least sensitive nose here as an amphibious mammal, and Aileen was just fine with that.

"Grav controls," she continued. "Currently set to about a quarter of what Humans are used to, so we can move things around."

"Fuel tanks are behind this wall and underneath about half this deck," Aileen gestured. "Generators are these three, and yes, I know that they are from three different manufacturers. The one on the right is original from when the ship was built. The other two are replacements for ones that died of old age or embarrassment."

Both Navy women snickered at her, but nodded.

"If you ran on different fuel sources, we could probably take two of them out and pull a spare from *Ajax*," H'Brige offered.

"Trust me, the thought has crossed my mind," Aileen chuckled. "And it would work all the time without leaking nearly as much."

Aileen found the toolbox right where Thadrakho had said he'd left it. Opening the top, she gestured the two engineers close.

"Feel free to inspect everything, but I'd suggest you not touch until Ereshkiki Nisab gets back," Aileen reminded them. Just in case.

"You're safe," Ishani laughed. "It would take longer than that to have it completely dismantled for cleaning anyway."

Aileen had to double-take to make sure the woman was kidding. She knew how unsupervised engineers could be.

But they could fix all this, if they could handle the more complicated stuff on *Ajax*. Only so many ways to do certain things. The trans-space drives were the only thing here really new to the women, and they'd get their chance to play with those after the ship was settled.

She headed aft to grab the sled and rolling sphere for the run back to *Ajax*, leaving the women here to do whatever they needed. Not too many trips and *Shiva Zephyr Glaive* would swap places with *Ajax* again.

Then the fun began.

TWELVE

ADDISON

ADDISON HAD GOTTEN detailed descriptions from Eha of all the High Council members of the Rio Alliance, as well as the woman/spy that was living a somewhat public relationship with Oluchi. All of them were gathered up as he emerged from the rear of the aircar that had transported him and Remahle south of Greenbriar, just as they had done with Eha before.

Hells, he hadn't had grass under his keel in more than a decade. So long that it felt wrong, which just told him that he needed to spend less time on a ship and more time on the ground. Maybe when this was all done, it would be time to sell the ship to Kuei for a beer and move on with his life?

Roald Cavalcanti was obvious as Addison got close. The tallest Human present and he possessed a charm that exuded from every pore and scale as Addison watched. Oluchi and the woman Anya were standing close to the Chair of the High Council, and everyone was surrounded by Council Guards who reacted more to Remahle than they did him, but they'd seen a Churquen before.

A Kr'mari was just another reminder of how complicated

Innruld Space could be. Forty different species sharing a small section of the galaxy, when the Human realms had less than a quarter of that.

Addison came to rest and coiled himself. A bow to the High Council, turning right to left. They returned it, but he could already sense the fracture lines in the nine facing him.

Eha had spent a decade as a spymaster. Her notes that he had memorized before leaving had been extremely detailed. Probably more than the Humans appreciated, as Eha had also told him that she felt like they were just patting her on the head scales more than once.

"Ambassador," the Chair said expansively. "Welcome back and congratulations."

"That belongs to Lazarus," he nodded to the man. "I was merely the messenger. But I do look forward to our discussions."

There. Let them understand that he wasn't really in the mood for another week spent discussing the shape of the table, rather than getting down to material tasks. Again, Eha had warned him what it had been like before.

She was also more inclined to patience than Addison was. Or perhaps, the time for patience was ending. Yes, that fit better his mood.

However, this group could not be budged from pomp, so he allowed them to guide him indoors to a catered reception.

Addison would have preferred the nice day outside, where there was a warm breeze and clear skies, things he had not dealt with much in years.

At least there was a patio.

After a time spent being introduced to everyone who could wrangle an invitation, he found himself out on the concrete slab, absorbing afternoon sun that had warmed it. If he were alone, Addison would have just stretched out and taken a warm nap.

What had happened to the teenager who might have done such a thing?

By some stretch of something Addison didn't believe for a moment was luck, he found himself alone with Oluchi Pryce and the Human woman who had gotten attached as...*something*. Remahle was the center of a group over there, hopefully not saying anything embarrassing for either of them.

"It is good to see you," Pryce said. "Is everything good back with the team?"

"It is," Addison nodded. "At least it was when I left. But as you know, that was when the hard part was going to begin."

Pryce nodded.

"I had dinner with one of the Councilors last night," the Human said. "Erlyn Teixeira. It was an informal sort of thing. A double date if you will, with Anya here and another woman. We talked about Eha's next steps."

The way he said it had Addison's tail kinked suddenly.

"What did you tell them?" he asked.

Lazarus and especially Eha had a high regard for this Human, but Addison hadn't spent that much time around him before now.

"Bluntly?" Pryce asked. Addison nodded. "That they had not all that long before Eha and maybe Lazarus decided that the Rio Alliance wasn't going to be a helpful ally against the Innruld, and that they needed to stop dithering and come to a conclusion. Not quite that bluntly, mind you, but I didn't soften the edge of the blade all that much either."

"Was that wise?" Addison asked.

He was a Director, not a diplomat, so he would have taken a different tack. At least he hoped so.

"Without Oluchi putting their feet to the fire, they

might spend a year not getting anywhere, sir," the woman spoke up now.

She hung on Pryce in a manner similar to how he and Eha were in public, so Addison assumed that they were a romantic item. Not that Addison would trust her until he and Pryce had a moment without minders to chat about the sorts of things Eha had filled in.

However, Eha had trusted the woman.

He had just spent too many years as a smuggler where any mistake with the kinds of cargo he hauled would simply get him executed out of hand. The Innruld had no sense of humor at all. Especially not for the narcotics the Species Underground delivered to Skycity hands.

Addison studied Anya Persaud with a sharp eye.

She seemed to want to be an ally. Gift horses and all that.

"Can they make a decision?" he asked her bluntly. "I won't wait a year. Eha won't, either. After commanding *Ajax* and watching Lazarus put the ship through a major battle, he won't need a year to topple the Innruld. The time for decisions is at hand. Let your masters know that."

She nodded, but it was more of a bow. Then she surprised Addison by nodding to Pryce and detaching herself from the man.

"I shall," she said simply, and then she was gone.

Just like that.

"Have I just provoked a crisis?" Addison asked, aware that he hadn't intended to chase the woman off.

Out of the corner of one eye he watched her walk to one of the Councilors, the one known as Teixeira, Addison thought, and whisper something in her ear.

"If you did, Addison, then they needed prodding," Pryce replied grimly. "I have tried to keep up the momentum that Eha had before she left, and have made some breakthroughs, but at some point we run into the surfeit of distrust."

"They don't know how weak the Innruld are?" Addison asked, a little surprised. "How easily Westphalia or Rio could step in and replace the masters if they wanted?"

"It was not my place to tell them, Addison," Pryce said in a stark enough tone that Addison turned back to stare at the Human from Yisan. Oluchi Pryce smiled and did that thing Humans did where his face turned red. "It is not my homeland that I would have been gambling with."

"Indeed, it was not," Addison replied. "But I wonder if playing that game much longer might entrap us all in the shadows until it is too late."

"Westphalia?" Oluchi asked.

"Lazarus had no doubts," Addison said, watching over Pryce's shoulder now as a small group of Humans began to approach, led by Persaud. "That suggests that they will find out as much as this government knows, possibly as fast as it does."

"Are you at risk?" Oluchi asked. "I was safe from threats because at the end of the day, I don't know anything dangerous."

Addison was rocked back onto his coil at that. He had been thinking of earlier when Eha was here with three Humans, of whom a dandy like Oluchi Pryce was the least dangerous. He had neither Grace nor Xiuying to protect himself against an assassin. And no idea which Humans might be inimical.

Persaud stepped close, bearing with her another Human woman, this one wearing formal robes. The others hung back at a polite distance.

Erlyn Teixeira. Possibly an ally. Possibly not. Certainly a center of power.

"Ambassador," Teixeira nodded as she got close, a wine glass in hand filled with an opaque crimson almost purple.

Humans and poisons.

"Councilor," Addison nodded back.

"A rumor suggests that you don't think there is much time to come to an agreement with the Rio Alliance," Teixeira offered.

"Oluchi and I were just discussing Westphalia, madam," he said. "And wondering how quickly their spies might have a transcript of all the conversations here tonight."

"It shouldn't be that quickly, should it?" she asked, glancing around with new eyes at the number of folks who might be here when they might not have been invited.

"Additionally, the curious possibility of an assassin," Addison added. "Eha had protectors she trusted with her life at Yisan. I have Oluchi, but he's not a warrior. Nor is Remahle, though he would dispute that with you."

Teixeira got serious.

"Should we move to a private room to chat?" she asked in a voice still cheerful, but with a hard tone underneath.

"Yes," Oluchi broke in suddenly. "And could you ask Councilors Cavalcanti and Martins to join us?"

Addison didn't grasp that significance, except that those two represented swing votes on the High Council frequently, with most of the others generally locked into ideological positions they might find it difficult to escape.

Addison allowed himself to be fawningly led back into the building and out of the sun he had been enjoying. The carpet in here was interesting, but not as nice as the grass. The smells were more the industrial scents of stations and less the surface of a planet.

He quickly found himself in a conference room. One that even had a good-enough approximation of a Churquen cone in it, so this must have been made for Eha while she was here.

Roald Cavalcanti and Ruby Martins joined Erlyn Teixeira

on the other side of the table, while he had Oluchi and Anya Persaud on his. Nobody else had come in.

Addison wondered how many listening devices might be present.

"You fear a threat to your person?" the Chairman asked in a supercilious voice. "We have Council Guards to protect us and the estate."

Addison fixed the man with a hard glare and flickered his pupils sideways just a little to remind the Human that he was a Churquen visitor.

"I could speak smooth, comforting words here, Humans," Addison began, maybe a little harder than Eha or Pryce would have. "Deflect things with niceties. But Oluchi reminds me that there are more significant problems at hand."

"Such as?" Teixeira asked, trying to smooth the waters from the two men roiling them.

"I must share a secret with you," Addison said. "Eha would not have, because she believed that negotiations would be successful, eventually. I have my doubts, although none of them coil around the three of you."

"What then, Ambassador Wolcott?" Teixeira pressed.

Addison took a breath and placed both hands flat on the table. He took a long glare at the three Humans and wondered, again, if history would start a chapter here or possibly end one. Maybe his entire trip to Human Space would make a section break in the history of the galaxy.

But Westphalia would not rest, once the truth known.

"When we rescued Lazarus, he had the clothes on his back because we accidentally destroyed the pincke he was flying at the time and he had to eject," Addison said. "That's my responsibility as Director of the ship and crew."

He watched them. They looked like small mammals

confronted by a poisonous reptile, to use the phrase he had picked up from Lazarus.

"It was only after taking command of *Ajax* that I learned a hard, cold, frightening truth, Human Councilors," Addison continued after a beat.

Again, none of them rose to the bait.

"Human technology is far in advance of Innruld," he admitted, wondering if he had just signed his death warrant.

But then, all Lazarus had to do was break the Innruld's hold. Addison Wolcott and Eha Dunham could fill a large transport with Churquen and disappear into deep space in the chaos. Maybe they would come closer to Human Space.

Maybe they would flee into the deeps instead.

He wouldn't need long, and the Churquen would be free. Addison felt a twinge of conscience at the others. Yithadreph. Vaadwig. Kr'mari.

They might all fall under the heel of a new oppressor, but give him a few generations and the help of Humans like Lazarus, and maybe the Churquen could return and free the entire galaxy from the Humans next, if that became necessary.

If he had to annihilate Westphalia, he could probably include the Rio Alliance for that price.

"How far?" Erlyn Teixeira asked after gasping.

"Far enough," Addison said succinctly. "If you chose to overthrow the Innruld, Humans could easily replace them as new overlords."

"Why are you telling us this?" the other woman, Ruby Martins, asked now.

"Because Westphalia will not hesitate to try, once they have the coordinates," Addison told her. "Possibly, even the right direction that they can send a few squadrons. Those two GunWalls that *Ajax* crushed at 6357 Wei Xiu would each be largely unstoppable with the technological sophistication they represent. Maybe a Innruld Pyramid could take one, but not a Security Barc by any stretch of the imagination."

"What could *Ajax* do?" Cavalcanti asked, the earlier aggressive bluster gone from his voice now. Possibly replaced with fear.

"*Ajax* with Lazarus in command could simply overthrow the entire Innruld structure," Addison replied. "That had been the plan from the start, perhaps with some help from the Rio Alliance. But your help is not necessary to win the war."

"What the Ambassador is trying to say is that you've probably already lost your chance to help Captain Oliveira defeat the Innruld, Councilors," Oluchi interjected. "What's left now is winning the peace that will come afterwards, when the Species Underground has to deal with Human warships in orbit of their worlds or preying on their shipping. Am I correct, Addison?"

"You are," Addison replied grimly. "Westphalia will eventually know which direction *Ajax* fled, but they'll have to look it up and recreate that first battle, because like you, they expected the ship to be destroyed. When it arrived at 6357 Wei Xiu, they discovered that it had not. When true aliens are found, sentient creatures representing a massive possible expansion of Rio Alliance space, they will be able to figure out where to go to do something about it."

"So you'll pull us into a war to protect your worlds?" Cavalcanti asked.

"You were already at war with Westphalia, High Councilor," Addison sneered at the man. "This is probably your chance to win it."

Addison paused for a long moment and stared hard at the Human.

"Or lose it."

THIRTEEN
RODRIGO

ADMIRAL RODRIGO DA SILVA was senior enough that sudden messages to turn over his command to Captain Quispe and report to *Fleet Base One* were a surprise. But it was Pedro Santos that had signed the order and Rodrigo suspected that things had probably gotten a little strange with the arrival of Commander Wolcott.

He snickered quietly.

The bureaucrats would have been expecting another one like Dunham or Pryce, when he could have told them that they were getting another *Pancho*.

So he grinned to himself as he emerged from the shuttle and returned the salute from the young lieutenant standing there in the station bay.

"Right this way, sir," the man said, turning and immediately stepping off.

Rodrigo didn't have to stretch his legs to keep up, but he couldn't dawdle either. The man led him to a doorway with two guards already in place, nodded, and stepped to the side. The new marines immediately keyed the door open, so Rodrigo entered.

It didn't surprise him to find Pedro here. Councilor Teixeira was unexpected.

Rodrigo felt the stakes go up quickly.

"Sit," Pedro said before Rodrigo was even fully in the room, so it wasn't going to be a formal ass-chewing.

You never knew when the system got stressed. People did weird, unforeseen things.

Teixeira was on his side of the table when he sat, but Rodrigo didn't put any great value on that. He'd only ever met her in passing at receptions, and probably never spoken to the woman beyond polite greetings even then.

But he'd known Pedro for decades, and the man was nervous. Tired, as well. Probably hadn't slept much in days from the bags under his eyes and the lines across his forehead.

Rodrigo waited, taking a moment to study the politician beside him. Amazingly attractive woman, considering that he knew her to be in her mid-sixties. Gray hair down to her shoulders. Green eyes. Dimples. Trouble, when you combined it with the sort of razor-sharp mind she had to have to be on the High Council.

"There have been developments, Admiral," she began, as if he would be surprised. "Interesting ones. Your name came up because the government might have seriously screwed up and needs the fleet to save us from ourselves."

Oh, goody.

Rodrigo had had a few of those in his life. Rarely did they make your career. More frequently they broke it, when you had to make impossible choices with minimal information, and others were grading you afterwards with the exactness of hindsight.

"Madam," he offered dryly, without any emotion or context, more as an acknowledgment that she was here than anything else. He probably wasn't going to enjoy this. Any of it.

At least she had the intelligence to smile at him, recognizing the gambit for what it was.

"What is your impression of Addison Wolcott?" she asked, going about where he expected her to.

He'd warned them.

Rodrigo wondered if anybody but Pedro had actually read the full report.

"For a 90-day wonder?" Rodrigo asked. She nodded. "Exceptional. But I put that down to his years as a private captain. A director, excuse me. The man knows command and ships. And didn't come across with any arrogance when faced with lifelong professionals. Why?"

Blunt. Possibly rude, even. Rodrigo da Silva wasn't feeling particularly interested in taking the fall for someone else's fuckup today.

"The government moved with the speed of bureaucracy, Admiral," she replied, surprising him with her honesty. "As is to be expected. The whole point of a civil service is to maintain equilibrium over time, tempering the worst of bad leaders and supporting the efforts of good ones."

"You waited too long," Rodrigo said. It wasn't even a guess. "*Pancho* took *Ajax* home and doesn't need you anymore."

"I find it interesting that you say *Home*, Rod," Pedro broke in. "He was born here on Brasilia."

"That crew was family, Pedro," he replied. "Weird shapes be damned. Just listening to them talk should have told you that. Weird, dangerous Human comes along and they don't eat him or put him in a zoo. Don't turn him over to the authorities and wipe their hands of the whole mess. No, they took him in. Gave him a job. Protected him from the Innruld. Went pirate when those folks came for him."

"How do you know that?" Teixeira asked.

"Aileen Enjehn was the key," he turned back to her. "She and I talked. That woman knew the entire logistical needs of *Ajax* off the top of her head. Knew what Human food the rest of her crew could eat and what to skip when loading supplies. From memory. You don't know those things if you don't care deeply. Lazarus was a baby brother to her."

She nodded at some internal commentary.

Rodrigo gambled now.

"Where did you screw up?" he asked the woman.

She turned hot for a second, then dialed it right back down to nothing as he watched. Might have even blushed a little.

"Admiral Santos did the right thing by sending Oliveira to Vilga to rout that Westphalian incursion," she said. "My allies helped Eha Dunham sneak out of the palace so she could be there, with the understanding that she would come back later."

"Except that she sent Commander Wolcott instead," Rodrigo completed the thought. "She's not coming back. Neither is *Pancho*. Am I right?"

He turned to Pedro and got enough of a nod to confirm that supposition.

"So where do I come in?" Rodrigo asked. "You didn't have me bring *Recife* into dock, so Paulo is handling the tub right now. At least until you put some other flag aboard her."

He would have normally enjoyed the pained expressions the other two shared. The commiseration. Except that he knew it was pointed at him.

He was about to get the short end of the stick.

Rodrigo shrugged. Not the first time. At least Pedro wasn't being an ass about it.

"Wolcott went about as perfectly far down the way of

threatening the High Council as you can get without actually doing it," Teixeira replied.

Impressive. Wolcott hadn't struck him as a diplomat. Maybe that had been Dunham's problem. She might have been too nice to the old shits to get their attention.

"What did he say?" Rodrigo asked, intrigued that someone had actually gotten the High Council to do something with any speed at all.

Maybe bad, but at least it was motion. Innruld Space needed to be dealt with now, not in a decade.

"Just exactly what you're thinking, Admiral," Teixeira replied. "We need to move."

"Hot damn," Rodrigo said. Then reality set in. "Oh, shit."

Yup. Pedro had *that* smile on his face.

"What have you done to me?" Rodrigo asked his superior officer with a sour voice.

"Addison is willing to haul a ship to Innruld Space, to help *Ajax*," Pedro said. "But only one, and under strictest secrecy."

"Why?"

It was educational, watching both of these politicians, one in uniform and one civilian, flinch.

"We screwed up." Councilor Teixeira was the one to speak.

"Oh?"

"We automatically assumed that Innruld Space was a new threat to Humanity, from a different direction," she continued.

"Makes sense," Rodrigo answered. "Forty new species in a political unit. What changed?"

"Two things," she said. "There are supposedly more Humans combined than all of the folks in Innruld Space, if Wolcott is to be believed, and I'm inclined to do so."

"How is that possible?" Rodrigo asked.

"The Innruld keep everyone else weak," she turned and stared squarely at him now, going so far as to turn sideways in her chair. "That means low numbers, crowding, small families. Just about the opposite of Humans, with so many new worlds to pick from. According to Wolcott, families of two are the single most common."

"Wow," Rodrigo said, contemplating his six siblings. "So stasis. What's the other problem?"

"He think we're at least a century more advanced than they are, technologically, if my experts did the math correctly," she said. "And again, static, while Humanity is developing rapidly as a result of the war."

"So when we would have found them in another century or three?" Rodrigo asked quietly.

"Europeans invading Amazonia like last time, Admiral," Pedro said in a hard, nasty voice.

All of them in the room were descended from the original colonists from the region of Brazil on the homeworld. It was a mix of ethnicities, and other worlds had joined one side or the other on something of an ethnic base. Westphalia was culturally and ethnically centered on northwestern Europeans, back on Earth, where Westphalia was a place.

Rodrigo hoped that the Rio Alliance would find an invasion as unsavory an outcome as he did. Maybe that was why they were here?

"That would explain a few things," Rodrigo offered. "Where do I fit in?"

"Wolcott doesn't trust the government, Admiral," Teixeira explained. "So we are willing to gamble pretty hard on this one. But at the same time, if he's right, Wolcott is pretty much putting himself at our mercy."

"One ship?" Rodrigo asked. "Which one?"

"A Patrol Cruiser," Pedro said. "One of the old Presidential boats. *Dutra*."

Rodrigo kept his profanity to himself.

The Presidential-class boats were named for ancient Presidents of the Brazilian Republic, back on Earth in history. They were something of a failed experiment, designed to have enormous sailing capacity by keeping the crew relatively small. At the same time, they sacrificed firepower as well, until they were barely more dangerous that a destroyer.

When *Dutra* worked, she could probably circumnavigate Rio Alliance Space and stop at every frontier world before needing to take on supplies. Rodrigo da Silva just didn't have any great expectations that they could sail anywhere near that far without something breaking down.

"I'll need more engineering crew members than you probably have aboard," he said, assuming it was a foregone conclusion at this point.

Pedro Santos could give him those orders, and resigning his commission in protest was about the only tool Rodrigo had to stop him. Of course, if he did that, he'd never see Innruld Space.

"You'll have it," Pedro said without a quibble. But then, he knew the reputation of those old boats as well. "We're also planning for you to capture Innruld boats and possibly bring them up to Rio tech levels, where possible, so you'll be crammed full with gear and extra crew as well."

"We going all in on this?" Rodrigo asked, a little shocked himself, given the reputation of the High Council for talking instead of acting.

"We have little choice at this point, Admiral," Councilor Teixeira replied. "As Wolcott pointed out, they don't need us, so we have to convince them that we still want to be friends. That they still want us as friends. They'll have *Ajax* to study at their leisure, and Captain Oliveira to help them jumpstart their technology."

"*Pancho* could do it," Rodrigo noted.

She nodded.

"That fear is exactly what finally broke through to the rest of them," she said. "And why we will have our work cut out for us."

"Us?" Rodrigo asked, unsure about the tone of her voice or the implications.

"Us, Admiral da Silva," she nodded again. "I'm coming with you."

FOURTEEN

LAZARUS

LAZARUS HAD to keep reminding himself that from here Kuei knew what she was doing way better than he did and he should just shut up. History would remember her as the person who opened this first pathway between the Species Underground and Rio Alliance Space, and she'd be excellent at it.

Akeley's Passage.

They'd left *Ajax* behind again. Lazarus felt the occasional twinge when he thought about it. To commemorate the occasion, he had dug out the crimson outfit with the beer logo on the chest, and ordered everyone who could to return to civilian clothing.

Luckily, they'd had stores of cloth on *Ajax* for whatever reasons, plus more they'd brought originally with them from *Shiva Zephyr Glaive*. Thadrakho was in heaven, spending all of his waking hours sewing, since Ereshkiki Nisab had enough engineers finally to keep the ship running.

The best part today was standing on the ship's tiny bridge and looking out the front window. Kuei was flying, with Cormac plugged in next to her. H'Brige was next to him, almost rigid with shock. Outside, everything was that pearlescent gray shot through with the strangest blues, because they were inside trans-space, a tunnel rather than a hole you could just step through.

She turned to him and he could see all seven tail feathers spread out like playing cards in someone's hand.

Lazarus smiled at her.

"I never…" she began, faltering into silence.

"The first time Addison explained it to me, I had a nervous breakdown," Lazarus replied. "They thought I was having a heart attack. Maybe I was. Hard to say."

"*Ajax* will utterly disrupt everything," she finally managed.

"It will," Lazarus agreed. "Now you see why we couldn't tell the folks back home how or where to find the Innruld."

"Then why did we leave the ship behind in the nebula?" H'Brige asked.

"Didn't have enough crew members to work both," he replied. "Had we not left everyone behind at Vilga's Stand, that would be a different story. As it is, we have to go connect with the Species Underground and recruit sailors we can train on the new technology. Plus, we've been gone for a while, so Eha needs to know what the Innruld have done in our absence."

"Would they do anything?" H'Brige asked. "You've said that Innruld Space is culturally static. Almost a dead end."

"Close," Lazarus corrected her. "A pedestal, with the Innruld at the top. Beneath that, their various servants who maintain the system for them. Then everyone else just trying to make a living. Change occurs, but nothing can ever be allowed that threatens to topple things."

"I've never been a revolutionary before," she offered in a small voice.

"You're a sailor," he reminded her. "The Rio Alliance

Navy exists to protect everyone from Westphalia. We've just extended our writ some here."

He heard a hatch open behind him and turned to see Eha emerge. It was Addison's office, configured for a Churquen, so he'd just brought over chairs from *Ajax* to sit on.

"Could I see you?" she asked.

Lazarus nodded and turned to H'Brige. Before he could speak, Eha interrupted.

"Both of you, actually," she amended.

Lazarus led, pulling a chair from a stack against the wall that would fit an Atomarsk's feathers, and then a second for him.

Eha waited for the door to close and took a deep breath. He could tell how stressed she was from the way her scales didn't all align flat.

"I've been thinking about Gowook," she began. "What we do or say when we get there."

"Hopefully, your face isn't on a wanted poster," Lazarus said. "But even then, you've got me, Grace, Lucas, and a dozen sailors who are all armed. Nothing can get to you without getting through us."

"Thank you," she said. "But I'm more worried about getting the movement to rise up. When you and I left, my orders had been to separate you from Addison so that they could interrogate you for intelligence value."

"Lucky for you that you failed, then," he said, trying not to sound too flippant as he did.

"Agreed," she countered. "But we'll have to get them to step past everything they originally thought and prepare them for the arrival of Humanity. Not everyone will want to believe the truth, even after I can swear to it from firsthand experience. Having an Atomarsk along will just push everything into the realm of fantasy for some of them."

"You think I'm at risk again?" Lazarus smiled,

contemplating the Underground trying to threaten him now, given everything he'd learned. "Us?"

Not that he was all that worried, with Grace around. He still wasn't entirely sure about the woman, but they'd started sharing a cabin. And sleep. And other things. Slowly. Haltingly, even, but getting there.

"The entire mission might be," Eha said. She sighed. "It might even be a fool's errand and we should have come with *Ajax* handy. Nothing could stand against that ship."

"I could offer some options, but many of them probably hinge on a willingness to use excessive violence," Lazarus turned serious now.

"My fear is that it becomes necessary, Lazarus," she said. "Especially if *Shiva Zephyr Glaive* is known to be a rebel ship. The authorities might decide to shoot first, rather than take their chances. At the very least, they might line up all their security troops and trap us in a dock."

"They tried that once, I might remind you," Lazarus said. "Didn't work out. But I have a suggestion I haven't shared with you yet. Something sneaky."

"Oh?"

"Let's steal a ship," Lazarus offered. "One they don't know about. Then we can park *Shiva Zephyr Glaive* for a while and run around in a different vessel until they figure it out."

"How?"

He turned to H'Brige.

"Reminder, your kind are legendary," he told the Atomarsk engineer. "Unicorns, if you will. If you show up and ask to talk, most ships will fall all over themselves to do so."

"The same way the Atomarsk first encountered Humans?" she smiled.

An Atomarsk private ship, a miner, alone in a distant

system minding his business when a Human exploration vessel appeared. And changed the future for both species.

Maybe all of them.

"Exactly," Lazarus said, turning back to Eha. "What if we change course right now and pop up at some dead-end station? One of the small ones, rather than a hub like Zhoonarrim or Dormell. An outpost, maybe with a small Security Barc?"

"What good would that do?" Eha asked, her scales crinkling up in yet greater confusion.

Lazarus laughed.

"You're a spy, Eha," he said around a huge smile.

"Well, yes."

"You've never been a pirate," he continued.

"And you have?" she challenged.

"Let us just say that you do not have the security clearance that would allow me to answer that question."

"Oh."

Lazarus grinned. This was going to be fun. And nothing at all like anybody had been expecting.

FIFTEEN

LUCAS

LUCAS WASN'T sure how he felt about the whole plan, but he was just a lieutenant. His job was to take orders from senior officers. Lazarus certainly qualified, even if everyone was pretending to be civilians now.

No, his concern was the robot. Cormac. A NavCrawler, like the other one—Lenox—was a MedCrawler. Fully sentient creatures based on silicon rather than carbon.

Manufactured life forms.

Nothing had prepared him for that.

Worse, for a robot with a sense of humor who cracked jokes. Pretty dirty ones, too.

Lucas was in the main office of the tiny ship, off the back of the bridge, with Lazarus and Cormac. It was mid-day ship's time. He was on first shift, with the crew split in two and hot bunking, just because otherwise they had too many people and not enough space to put them all.

"Questions?" Lazarus asked as he finished explaining the plan.

Lucas wanted to ask "Will it work?" but he knew that was a useless thing at this point. It would or it wouldn't. If it did, fine. If it didn't, they would have to piece something together as they went.

Or go back and get *Ajax*. There were no problems you couldn't solve with a big enough hammer.

Lucas just remembered his instructors telling him that every problem wasn't necessarily a nail.

"Can we man a Security Barc?" he asked instead. "Fight from it?"

"Doubtful, Lucas," Lazarus said as Cormac pivoted a camera probe this way to study him. "*Ajax* was designed for automation, while the Innruld generally are the opposite in almost everything."

"Sir?"

"*They believe in having servants do the work so the masters don't have to,*" Cormac spoke up. "*Lesser life forms, all the way down to electronic ones such as myself. We were an experiment in subservience.*"

"Were?" Lucas asked after he got over the flash of anger at building an entire government that way.

"*In order to make us successful, they had to keep increasing our cognitive abilities.*" Cormac's voice seemed filled with humor. "*Eventually, they just added another servant species. Otherwise, they would have had to do work, instead of ordering someone around. Many have not forgiven the inventor of the Crawler for that failure.*"

"Failure?" Lucas asked, confused.

"*Now we have to have rights allotted to us,*" Cormac laughed. "*Rather exactly the opposite of what the Innruld originally intended. That's why they stopped making Crawlers for the most part.*"

"Oh," Lucas saw it now. "Won't the Innruld do something when they see you, then?"

"*I am beneath Innruld contempt, Lucas,*" Cormac replied. Wow.

He turned back to Lazarus now and understood that light in the commander's eyes finally. Just one more species for Westphalia to oppress when they got here.

If they got the chance.

Those bastards would have to go through him first to get there.

"And you think Thadrakho is up to it?" Lucas asked.

"He's incredibly intelligent, Lucas," Lazarus replied. "I would say lazy, but that's the wrong word. His kind live in nests in an ice world, with everything directed by a queen. What Thadrakho needs is a set of instructions he can follow to give his life shape."

"Like making clothes," Lucas gasped.

"According to Aileen, he's never been so happy as having to sew all the time, instead of trying to figure out what part of *Shiva Zephyr Glaive* had broken most recently and what he should try to fix first. Humans tend to enjoy that sort of a challenge in ways that would make a Necherle's skin crawl, if their skin was on the outside of the chitin."

Lucas took a breath. He'd never been a pirate, but he could be a cop. Protecting the weak from the predatory.

And maybe he'd run into a mouthy Innruld one of these days. Lazarus had said that the so-called masters of the galaxy were amazingly tall, incredibly beautiful, and utterly fragile creatures.

Maybe he'd get the chance to bounce one of those annoying shits off a bulkhead sometime soon.

SIXTEEN
H'BRIGE

SHE WASN'T sure she was prepared to impersonate a diplomat, but H'Brige was willing to try. And Lazarus and Eha had both agreed that the sort of place they were going would be falling all over themselves in the excitement of meeting an Atomarsk in the flesh.

She just had to pull it off long enough for the others to get involved.

Having a Vaadwig on the bridge with her was acceptable, according to the legend they were building. Humans and Churquen were the ones who could not be seen, lest someone recognize Eha or the tales of alien visitors.

Thadrakho was acting as Director today. Kuei was flying. Cormac and Wybert were aft. Everyone else was hiding.

Necherle were tall. Thadrakho was even taller than Lazarus by a few fingers. The species were cold adapted and insectile, with four multi-faceted eyes arranged in two pairs top and bottom above the mouth. Their mandibles worked sideways, rather than vertically, and tended to clack quietly when he was focused. Or nervous, like now.

Instead of ears, he had four antennae emerging from the

top of his skull, on each of the four corners of his round head. Each pointed outwards at thirty degrees and were largely immobile, but allowed him to sense, hear, and smell with great precision.

Thadrakho was covered over with chitin plate protecting everywhere like a suit of armor, and he had a tail that ended in a spiked tip almost as dangerous as his claws. Except that Thadrakho was more likely to poke himself with a needle than draw blood on someone else.

They were born for the ice, so he tended to walk in short, mincing steps, using his tail as a tripod frequently.

H'Brige would have called him an ice demon, but again, he'd have to be dangerous first. She'd had Human kittens who were more of a threat. This big, skinny, pencil of a bug was just impersonating a director because Eha had told him to. Her gender, and H'Brige's, meant that he saw them as queens to be obeyed.

Weird, but she could work with it.

"Stand by for emergence," Kuei announced. "Fifteen seconds."

H'Brige took one long, last look at the inside of a hyperspace tunnel and wondered if it would be a technology worth improving. Star drives were faster, but you went point to point each time in a perfectly straight line that could not pass through a gravitational well. Trans-space drives let you turn corners. They were slow, but more maneuverable.

Tomorrow's problem. She had a play to stage today.

She turned to Thadrakho.

"Ready?" she asked.

His face was immobile, but he clacked his jaw once and blinked all four eyes. That was a good sign.

Shiva Zephyr Glaive dropped into real space.

"How far out are we, Kuei?" Thadrakho asked in a voice that even sounded impressive and deliberate.

"Twice the usual distance and quite a bit high," the Vaadwig woman replied. "Didn't want to look too professional here."

H'Brige shared a laugh with the others. Nobody had a particularly high opinion of what they might expect out here at Onunk, but it only took one pain-in-the-ass Innruld, perhaps an exile from a prominent family with education and an attitude problem, to cause the whole plan to fail.

She'd served under a few officers like that in her career.

"Contact the station," Thadrakho commanded in as strong a voice as he could.

The man had a role to play, and a script. And she could step in if she had to. Or Kuei.

Hopefully it wouldn't be necessary.

Kuei did something on her board and got a cheerful beep back.

"How long?" she asked, unsure what *normal* looked like in Innruld Space.

"We're about two light-seconds out right now," the Vaadwig woman replied, rotating her head back over her shoulder like a Terran owl. "And I don't expect them to react quickly. Or rather, I expect panic at their end, and a lot of flailing until they remember to answer."

H'Brige nodded. She focused on keeping her tail feathers fanned out just a little. Normally they did that when she was stressed. Or showing off for a male. Here, it would reinforce that she was a unicorn.

An Atomarsk, when nobody had supposedly seen one in centuries or longer.

Nothing happened for so long that H'Brige began to wonder if the station was asleep.

Thadrakho apparently felt the same way.

"Lay in and execute an approach course," he said

suddenly, sounding nothing at all like himself, but instead like stories she'd heard about Addison Wolcott.

Kuei must have felt the same way, because she looked back in surprise, shrugged, then began typing on her board.

Shiva Zephyr Glaive began to shift, until H'Brige finally saw the station.

She couldn't help the gasp of surprise. She'd seen images of Zhoonarrim and Dormell, immense cities floating in orbit, housing thousands of permanent residents.

Onunk Station was smaller than *Ajax*. Maybe about the same amount of metal, reshaped into something only a few hundred yards across and maybe six decks tall total, depending on clearance.

"Yup," Kuei laughed. "Welcome to the tip of the tail, where it drags in the mud and yuck."

"What's the permanent staff on a station that size?" H'Brige asked. She'd heard it before, and the reality had pushed it right out of her mind again.

"Maybe a thousand," Thadrakho answered instead of Kuei. "It is not a cargo destination, but a customs port. There is one Security Barc docked, two freighters of medium size, and a handful of smaller vessels such as ours."

H'Brige couldn't tell, but Thadrakho was all about details. She trusted his judgment.

"*MA-44320*, this is Onunk Control," a voice finally got around to calling them back, after Kuei had engaged her engines and started inward. "You claim to have encountered an alien species and interacted with it. What lies are these?"

"Kuei, please activate the wide-angle camera and begin beaming an image to the station," Thadrakho said in a pleased voice. Again, he had a script to follow.

"Go," Kuei said.

"Onunk Station Control, this is *MA-44320*, Director Thadrakho speaking," he said, only lying about the name of the ship at this point. "Which part of the previous message did you find confusing?"

Shiva Zephyr Glaive had a projection screen that could be called up, as well as local stations for everyone. H'Brige got to watch their eyes as they realized that Thadrakho hadn't been lying to them when he said he had brought an Atomarsk Ambassador to Onunk.

It was just the rest of it that would be a surprise. If everything went right.

Gasps. Shock. Bedlam.

Lazarus and Eha had been right, though. That was an Innruld. Male. Amazingly beautiful in an androgynous way, with a long chin and high cheekbones. Eyes were a solid color, a golden-blue with no whites. Fine blond hair hung down in a loose, wind-blown manner that must have taken him an hour every morning to achieve, from what she knew about hair from Humans.

And that was her cue.

"I am Ambassador H'Brige Slani," she announced in a pleasant voice. "Atomarsk, as you can see."

Just to rub it in, she flared all her feathers out like there was a cute Atomarsk male over there to see them.

"Are you the appropriate representative of Innruld Space with whom I should be speaking?" H'Brige asked, pulling her tail back to a single blade now.

"Atomarsk," the man whispered like he was in pain.

Not exactly the response a woman wants out of a strange male who has just seen her feathers in all their glory, but he was Innruld. A Philistine, to use Lazarus's favorite non-profane term.

"That is correct," H'Brige hammered on him some more. "Atomarsk. This vessel encountered mine in deep space, and the Director agreed to transport me here. Was that a mistake? Should we head somewhere more important?"

From his reaction, the Innruld had never been slapped, physically or verbally. Never *thwarted*.

He didn't like the feeling. A flash of anger appeared for just a moment.

"No," he commanded. "We will rendezvous with you and bring you to the station, so that you can be properly conveyed to the Innruld authorities."

The man cut the line without waiting for an answer. Thadrakho did the same a moment later and turned to look at her. All four eyes flashed big for a moment and then blinked. He opened an intercom.

"Phase One is complete and successful," Thadrakho announced. "We will have visitors shortly."

H'Brige could hear faint cheering coming up the hallway from the cargo area that made up the ship's belly.

"Kuei, park us just outside the outer markers," Thadrakho instructed. "Wouldn't want to be close enough to them to be a threat."

He turned to her again and bowed formally, which just looked weird when his tail went horizontal to provide balance, like a gray T-Rex.

"Ambassador, we are now ready for the next stage of the mission," Thadrakho announced with a chuckle.

H'Brige hoped that he was right.

SEVENTEEN
LAZARUS

LAZARUS HAD EMPTIED out the arms and storage locker just to the right of the main airlock in order to stuff bodies in there. Most of the Humans were in there with him, hidden, with Grace closest to the door and then him and Lucas. Battery Commander Afolayan and his gunners were crammed in the back. Singh and her people were hiding in Addison's cabin forward, with Eha.

Nobody strange would be visible except H'Brige.

He glanced down at Cormac, illuminated by the thin slice of light coming from the barely-open door.

"Prepared for mayhem?" he asked the Crawler.

"*Affirmative, Director,*" the bot answered in a chipper voice.

Lazarus leaned close to Grace. Closer. Against her. Only partly to enjoy the touch of her skin. He also needed to whisper.

"You ready?" he asked.

She turned a bright, sarcastic smile his way and kissed him on the tip of the nose.

Not quite a pat on the head, but close enough. Lazarus chuckled with the rest of the boarding team.

He hoped they didn't have to board the ship. If this worked, the crew over there would handle things themselves.

Rude, but nobody would have to get hurt. Not even the ones that deserved it.

The ship jarred just a little as the Security Barc docked and extended their boarding tunnel with a clunk that went all the way through the hull.

Lazarus was tall enough to see over Grace's head, so he could see Wybert, Thadrakho, and H'Brige standing out in that same spot Addison had been when he first got rescued by this crew.

So much has changed.

Wybert still had his powerspear, but it was his teddy bear. He also had a pair of beam pistols strapped across the bottom of his thorax where a biped would have hips. He had even stripped the tan paint off his breastplate, taking it back down to the turquoise it had been that day.

Beeping sounded as the airlock began to open. Air pressure blinked hard once as it normalized back down to the level Innruld felt comfortable with.

They also wouldn't appreciate the gravity in here, turned up to 1.05g and comfortable for Human sailors, when Innruld Space generally ran at 0.8g.

It would throw all your reflexes off.

Tromp of booted feet. Gasps of surprise audible even above that. Sounded like three people, which would be about what Lazarus would have expected. One Innruld and two goons. The only question would be what species were serving as brutes today, and how quickly they would be willing to surrender.

Nobody had a stun weapon capable of effortlessly taking forty species down without harm. Lazarus and his folks had brought beam weapons capable of destruction instead.

"Ambassador," a smooth tenor voice spoke now. Presumably the Innruld himself.

Lazarus wondered how many Innruld officers there might be here. Not more than a handful at most had been Eha's estimate. This station was the ass end of beyond in more ways than one.

"I am H'Brige Slani," she said loudly. "Who would you be, sir?"

"Kraiusu Uryuon," the man replied. "Customs official for Onunk Station. Welcome to Innruld Space. No one has seen an Atomarsk in living memory. Where do your people come from?"

Lazarus listened with half an ear as H'Brige began spinning a most elaborate fable pointed in exactly the wrong direction, except that someone coming from that part of the galaxy might just conceivably end up encountering a ship outwards from Onunk.

At the same time, Grace was slowly moving the hatch from the nearly-closed position to open. H'Brige would have used different language to give Grace a warning, so presumably the two goons with Uryuon were too mesmerized by her presence to do their jobs correctly.

Not that Lazarus minded.

He leaned back and nodded at the others. They were all set.

Addison or Eha would be aghast, but Humans took violence for granted. Lazarus didn't like to dwell on the implications of that, though.

Grace leaned out and began to move, so silent and slippery that she was gone before Lazarus realized it. Cormac moved on freshly-oiled axles in her wake.

Lazarus had his favorite Ares pistol in hand as he slipped

into the hallway. H'Brige and the other two were almost back in the main cargo dome, and the three intruders had walked all the way over there to chat with them as H'Brige talked about the importance of turning Onunk into a new trade center for Atomarsk-bound ships and how rich everyone was going to get.

Lazarus was halfway to Grace and held there, watching the Innruld. She could handle her job without his help. He just didn't have to like that she didn't need him.

Or maybe he did. With a woman like Grace, that meant that she chose him, which actually made it better.

He smiled broadly as Chief Afolayan slid up next to him and the others oozed out of the locker room.

H'Brige was doing something with her tail to flair it out and then return it to rest, so her audience was rapt.

Now it was time for the interesting bits.

EIGHTEEN

GRACE

GRACE HELD her dark face calm and innocent, just as her teachers had always drilled into her. The geisha never let her raw emotions appear on the surface, but always projected that thing most guaranteed to calm someone. As an assassin, such acting skills also helped, when she needed to get close to someone.

She had never considered starship piracy as a vocation, but Eduardo had instructed her to protect Lazarus and Eha. She was doing that, and what she did in her spare time wasn't anything she expected that Eduardo would find objectionable.

It was still far beyond anything the man had envisioned when they had gotten a call about a kidnapping...

She allowed herself a faint smile, listening to Slani spin her fables. The Atomarsk was a good storyteller. She had rhythm to her words that drew the listener, and Grace had been trained to hear it and replicate that.

At her feet, the boxy robot named Cormac the NavCrawler had reached the corner of the airlock and stuck a tiny probe in at ankle level, where it was unlikely to be noticed.

While Humans were extremely tall, relative to most species, the rest were closer to Aileen and Remahle. Their eyes would be at her chest level if she did the same.

Cormac moved on silent wheels, entering the airlock and rolling.

Hearing nothing, Grace followed a moment later.

The Innruld had opened the airlock and a short tunnel from their ship to create a walkway about fifteen feet long. And then hadn't bothered securing the far end against someone just walking in. Presumably, the three behind her weren't supposed to get that deep into a ship needing inspection.

She had Lazarus and the other Humans behind her now, so Grace could focus on the corridor in front of her, letting Cormac get a sizable lead as he trundled quietly down one edge, letting her stay to the other.

The smells emanating from down there became clearer as Grace got closer, but there was still just a little bit of a breeze from behind her, since *Shiva Zephyr Glaive* kept its internal pressure closer to where Humans preferred it.

But the Security Barc, as they were called, stank. The smell of sour food rotting somewhere, mixed with bodies that had not showered frequently enough, to create a tang that almost made her eyes water. Toss in the hint of old grease that has turned crusty and she had the impression of poverty.

Maybe of the soul, since the Innruld were wealthy, but they hadn't wasted a single pfennig on keeping their ship clean and well-founded. She felt a moment of deep offense at the whole thing, and wondered if they should keep some prisoners behind just to put them to use cleaning everything, but she doubted they could be trusted.

No, better to have everyone familiarize themselves by taking this ship apart and putting it back together correctly.

Cormac had reached the end of the tunnel and looked both ways with that anklecam of his. He turned it to look at her with the prearranged signal that someone was there that might notice a Crawler suddenly appearing, so she stepped close. He gestured to the right.

Grace glided against the edge of the frame and slowly slid into sight, to see someone doing maintenance on an open panel maybe eight feet away. He had a toolbox at his feet and as she watched, the creature knelt and began rooting around for a tool. If she understood Eha correctly, the species was Aknaan. About five feet tall and bipedal, but birdlike, with legs hinged backwards like a chicken and arms that came almost to its ankles, wrists covered over with downy feathers in gray. The uniform was the same turquoise of the three behind her, but this one wore coveralls. The face had a beak similar to H'Brige, short and strong for crushing nuts rather than the long thin one a hummingbird had.

It looked light. Fragile. Punching it as hard as she might a Human would probably be lethal, but Grace had no idea where the soft parts might be that could easily disable it.

She would risk physical violence. It was one person, and he wore an enemy uniform.

Grace leaned back as the creature looked down and exploded into action.

The Aknaan started to turn towards her, seeing movement out of the corner of any eye. His beak dropped open in shock, and then she shut it with a hard fist, following that with an elbow into the forehead. On most creatures, the space just above the eyes was the spot best designed to take an impact.

She hoped that a solid concussion would be the only result.

Certainly, the creature went over backwards and lay still on the deck. She knelt and placed a hand on its chest. Heart still beating, so hopefully she hadn't just killed her first alien.

She looked back to see Cormac come around the corner and quickly telescope a plugin probe up to about two feet off the deck.

He plugged in, beeped once, and every alarm on the Innruld ship went off.

NINETEEN

LAZARUS

LAZARUS and his gunners were all set for violence, but he'd never realized how quickly an Ilount could move when he wanted.

The alarms on the Innruld ship started and Wybert did a cowboy-fast quick draw from both holsters, covering the two guards with the official.

"Drop your weapons or die," he ordered in a squeaky voice that didn't seem to be asking.

A year ago, Wybert would have probably looked comical doing that.

Today, he looked carnivorous. The two goons, a Vaadwig male and Yithadreph male, decided to survive and dropped their rifles.

"What's going on?" the Innruld demanded.

Lazarus exploded off the wall, coming right up behind the man and rabbit-punching him. It was a weird motion, because the man was seven and a half feet tall, so Lazarus hit him with a solid right cross into the kidneys instead of an uppercut.

Fool went down hard and fast.

"I've got this," Wybert announced.

Lazarus took a look at the Fusilier and decided that maybe he did.

"Let's go," Lazarus said to the Humans as he turned and raced for the airlock.

Cormac had reached into their computer system and set off all the engine overload alarms, followed a moment later by the call to abandon ship.

The NavCrawler was standing in the airlock hatch when he got there.

"*She went forward, Lazarus,*" the NavCrawler called above the din, pointing to his left.

Lazarus turned to Afolayan.

"Secure Engineering," he ordered the man. "Take your whole team. I'll support Grace."

"She gonna need help?" the man drawled.

"Grace might not even need me," he laughed. "I'm just backup."

"On it, sir," he said.

The gunners pounded aft while he moved forward.

This was a small ship as security vessels went. At the low end of cost, with everything on a single deck, rather than some of the monsters you might find at big stations.

To Lazarus, it reminded him of a simple Patrol Cutter back home. Customs Enforcement and occasional Search and Rescue. Two hallways running parallel lengthwise, with offices and shops in the middle and crew quarters along the outside.

He left behind the unconscious Aknaan mechanic who had apparently been Grace's first victim and started to jog. At the first intersection, he found a Kreeghal flat on his face, so Lazarus presumed that she had taken his advice and hit the man as hard as she could, rather than settling for subtle.

Kreeghal were about the only people in Innruld Space Lazarus worried about, from a physical standpoint.

The entire hull rocked once and shimmered like an earthquake. Hopefully, that was the aft escape pod firing, just like you were supposed to do when the call came to abandon ship. Everyone jumps in, settles in your assigned space, and closes the hatch once you have everyone accounted for.

According to Aileen and others, a ship like this would have first and second watch, with the day crew presumably on duty now and the night team asleep aft. Those off duty would have been fastest to go, easiest to account for.

The bridge hatch was open. Another Aknaan was standing there with his wings in the air, next to a Kdari, the leotaur like he had seen in that tea shop poetry slam, once upon a forever ago.

Grace had a pistol aimed at them when he entered, and a second one pointed at him until she identified that it was Lazarus coming.

"Keep them covered," he said, dropping right down into the pilot's nest. The Innruld's command throne behind him wouldn't have any controls for anything. They had staff to order around for that.

Quickly, he looked around the security cameras, but there was nobody moving in the hallways right now. Afolayan and his three were standing in engineering, threatening a Mizanet, the same sort of slug that had owned the tea shop on Zhoonarrim.

"The ship is secured!" he yelled over the address system. "Cormac, turn everything off, please. Afolayan, he'll walk slow, but bring him forward."

Instantly the alarms ceased and Lazarus found he could think again. He turned to his two prisoners.

"We're Humans," he announced in Interlac, the common Innruld tongue everyone here spoke. "Don't do anything stupid right now and we won't have to kill you. You'll go into the other lifeboat as soon as I can round everyone and jettison it. Understand me?"

The Kbari had more stripes on his uniform. He nodded carefully. Lazarus rose and opened the lifepod lock.

"You wait in there while I go get all your companions," he ordered.

Grace just smiled and actually blew a kiss at him as he went by. She really just needed him to fly the ship. Possibly, she could have snuck in without Cormac and ambushed all of them, given time.

Just one of the reasons that woman frightened him.

And aroused him.

Lazarus grabbed the unconscious Kreeghal first and tossed the heavy man over a shoulder fireman style before returning to the bridge and putting him down in the open pod. The Aknaan was next. The Mizanet engineer moved like a slug on his monopod, but Lazarus was already familiar with the species, so he crossed over to where Wybert still covered the other three.

The Innruld hadn't gotten up off the deck, but Wybert was using his upper arms to hold his powerspear on the man while his lower arms held blasters on the guards. H'Brige and Thadrakho had taken the beams from the guards and covered them now as well.

"You three, time to abandon ship," Lazarus ordered.

The Innruld grumbled until Wybert activated the powerblade with a sharp hum, then the official rose and towered over all of them.

"You'll all pay for this," he hissed angrily at them.

Lazarus wasn't in the mood. He grabbed the fellow by the lapels and pulled him down to eyeball level. It helped that he outweighed the skinny punk.

"You're going into the lifeboat with the others," he

snarled at the Innruld. "If I were you, I'd be more worried about whether the rest of your crew took a vote and decided that you never made it home alive. Am I clear?"

The two goons had stiffened at the implications, but didn't seem in a hurry to meet their Maker.

Lazarus got them all forward to the bridge and into the lifepod, about the time the Kreeghal and the unconscious Aknaan finally started to recover.

Everyone was strapped in, glowering in anger or cowering in fear as they looked out at him.

"Arm the pod," Lazarus ordered the Kbari in a cold voice.

The man nodded again, never having spoken, and Lazarus stepped back. Hatch locks closed and sealed.

A moment later, the lifeboat fired, rocking the entire ship like the wake of a big ship passing.

Lazarus looked around. Everyone involved in violence was here, with the rest back on *Shiva Zephyr Glaive* hiding or waiting.

"Okay, we've turned pirate," he told his crew with a hard smile. "Now we need to go liberate everyone from the Innruld."

They cheered, but it was a harsh sound. More like wolves growling.

Lazarus was looking forward to the next part.

TWENTY

EHA

SHE DIDN'T QUITE UNDERSTAND the logic. Eha knew they'd stolen a small Security Barc, but wasn't sure how they would hide that as she listened to a more-technical explanation than she could follow.

They were aboard the new ship now, in trans-space headed to a quiet corner where they could leave *Shiva Zephyr Glaive* for a time. She, Lazarus, and Aileen on the Barc, with Cormac flying and Kuei and Ereshkiki Nisab, while everyone else was aboard *Shiva Zephyr Glaive* following.

The commander's office was the only room she'd found so far that didn't have a rank smell of unwashed bodies. It was decorated with a clean carpet and fresh, mauve paint on the walls, as well as several portraits of severe-looking Innruld officers. The desk was clean and unlocked, containing a few interesting papers Eha was planning to go through later. The man's chair had been chucked out an airlock even before they left.

At least the Human engineers had been aggressively insulted by the state of the ship and were in the process of cleaning everything. Possibly within an inch of its life, given the growls she'd heard.

Lazarus and Aileen had nerded completely out as they sat there, like they did when they forgot anyone else was around, so she thwapped her tail on the deck once.

They turned to her, perhaps a bit embarrassed.

"Will it work?" Eha asked them as they both blushed in their own ways.

"Absolutely," Lazarus said. He started to explain technical details again and she pointedly turned to Aileen.

"There are a set of transmitters aft," Aileen said, putting a hand on Lazarus's arm to silence him. "We can change them around to something else and the folks at Gowook won't know that this ship used to be theirs. These little vessels aren't nearly as standardized as Pyramids and the large stations. We'll be fine, Eha."

"Good enough," Eha sighed. "I'm well beyond anything I ever imagined I'd be doing with my life or rebellious tendencies. We just land on Gowook like a freighter and go?"

"Yacht," Lazarus said succinctly. "You can play the role of a wealthy somebody returning home from wherever after however long. You and Aileen contact the right folks, and we can start your war."

"My war?" Eha gasped. "This is not my war."

"Yes, it is," Lazarus said. "I was just a sailor trying to get home. Addison was just a Director nibbling at the edges of the foundations of Innruld Space. You were the one that convinced me and the rest of us that we needed to go on the offensive. To bring down the Innruld. I'm just quietly happy that Addison is back in Rio Space."

"Why is that?" Aileen turned to him with a quizzical face, but Lazarus was looking at Eha.

"Eha would be happy overthrowing the Innruld," Lazarus

said, flickering his eyes to Aileen and back. "Addison wouldn't have stopped there, would he?"

Eha let her grimace speak for her.

"Eha?" Aileen asked.

"He's right," the Ambassador replied. "Addison might have taken *Ajax* and started hunting the Innruld, all of them, instead of just breaking them."

"They do have it coming," Aileen offered weakly.

"We all have it coming," Lazarus corrected her. "But I have another question, Eha."

"Yes?"

"Were you also looking at starting colonies in Human Space?" Lazarus asked. "The places *Ajax* visited while you and I were at Brasilia are all semi-terraformed, but supposedly uninhabited."

"Look at the Moah or Gnashiiley," she gestured with one hand. "In Rio Space, they are taller, stronger, maybe more robust than they are in Innruld Space. At this point, they might even be a different species completely, having been isolated for so long."

"And?" he asked.

"And why shouldn't the Churquen have that option?" Eha countered. "The Yithadreph? The Vaadwig? The rest?"

Lazarus nodded with recognition.

"Let's not mention that to too many Humans, shall we?" he grinned. "I had always assumed that you were going to run into the deep darkness and hide."

"That was the original plan and we might have to do that as well," Eha said. "What we needed, the whole of the Species Underground, was for the Innruld to be challenged at least long enough for colony ship projects to sneak off. Our original hope was that Humans could distract the Innruld for that stretch, not realizing what a threat Humans might actually be to everything."

"Which option appeals to you, Eha?" Lazarus asked. "I'm just the muscle here. *Ajax* is just a tool. You are the Ambassador, but you can also be the Churquen High Councilor who makes decisions for some slice of Innruld Space and the Species Underground. Same with Aileen and the Yithadreph."

"Hey, now," Aileen barked angrily. "What are you talking about?"

"Politics," Eha spoke the word like a curse. "We can't ask everyone involved, so it becomes necessary for us to become representatives of this future government we want to create, and make decisions that will benefit the largest number of sentient beings."

"At the same time, the Innruld don't get a vote at all," Lazarus added. "At least not until you decide to allow them to. You are at war and they are a different government."

"The Rio Alliance," Aileen gasped.

"Exactly," Lazarus replied.

Eha quoted it before he could.

"Quando no curso de eventos Humanos..."

"When in the course of Human events..."

Aileen's ears were all the way back, but she didn't blame the woman. She knew that Aileen wanted to play with three dimensional puzzles for a living, not make life and death decisions for people she'd never meet.

"Why me?" Aileen asked with a little bit of a wail to her voice.

"Someone has to," Eha said soothingly. "And you're a good person."

Lazarus nodded when she looked up at him, but she could see the dark thoughts in his eyes. Not that she blamed him. They were all being called upon to go beyond themselves.

"So what does that mean?" Aileen finally asked.

"I'd like you to be the Director of this ship," Lazarus said. He turned to Eha. "It will need a name at some point."

"Director?" Aileen asked. "Me?"

"Yes," he said. "Eha is the owner. Kuei will be your pilot once we rendezvous, just like on *Shiva Zephyr Glaive*, but the Humans all have to remain out of sight."

"Crap," she grumbled. "I hate it when you're right."

Aileen sighed and slumped a little.

"Hey," Lazarus poked her. "We'll still be there if you need a rescue. Won't have Xiuying, but Grace and I can do pretty good. Plus we'll have more friends and a Security Barc if they piss me off."

"Are you really going to upgrade the main gun?" Eha asked, reminded of some of the modifications that had been suggested at a previous meeting.

"Absolutely," he smiled. "We brought a spare Star Spear and a couple of generators we can install. There will be times when we need a bigger hammer to handle the job, at least until I go get *Ajax* and bring her in with a full Species crew."

Eha felt the same shivers she saw pass through Aileen, but they were both civilians.

Lazarus was right that this was going to be a war before it was all said and done. He and *Ajax* would carry them a tremendous distance, but at some point the Churquen, the Yithadreph, and the others would have to reach out and take what they wanted from the Innruld.

Whether the masters of the galaxy liked it or not.

TWENTY-ONE

RODRIGO

THE PATROL CRUISER *DUTRA*.

Rodrigo was at least pleased that his quiet, stubborn demands for engineers, support, and spare equipment had been taken seriously by Pedro Santos. The existing crew had grumbled some at first, since this class was designed to run with such a small crew that every person had a private berth but now they had to hot bunk and share.

Then they realized that there was budget to fix everything that had been beyond them for so long. And staff with nothing better to do than repair and replace broken and worn out gear.

Rodrigo doubted that *Dutra* had run this well at any point since it had completed Builder's Trials, about the time he was first commissioned.

The bridge was crowded. More so with a cone added for Wolcott and a nicer jumpseat installed for Councilor Teixeira. And a spare admiral with nothing better to do than take the blame for whatever went wrong. *Let us not forget that part.*

Rodrigo turned to Captain Carlos Nguema and grinned. The man was a Gnashiiley with a Human name. Tall for his kind, around five foot eight, so only a little shorter than Rodrigo was. Reddish-brown fur. Fluffy tail. Long slender face with white jaw fur, a long snout, and a black nose that had reminded everyone of a fox, to the point that their unofficial nickname back home was *Kitsune*, referencing an ancient Japanese legend.

Rodrigo still thought they looked more like red pandas, but nobody asked him.

"Are we ready to sail?" Rodrigo asked Nguema.

He appreciated the way that the Captain took a long, circular look around the bridge, with more than a dozen people stuffed in here right now. Including a spare Admiral, an extra High Councilor, and Commander Addison Wolcott, back in uniform in spite of his objections.

Dirty little secret there, when the High Council refused to accept his resignation and issued an emergency proclamation keeping him in harness. Addison hadn't bitched too much, since it was getting him the thing he needed.

Help.

"We are ready, Admiral da Silva," Nguema replied in a neutral voice. "Would you like to say a few words?"

"Personally, no. Commander Wolcott, would you?" Rodrigo turned to the Churquen.

Wolcott's hesitation was probably too small for others to identify, but Rodrigo had spent a lot of time in the man's presence over the last few weeks, planning everything out. Aileen Enjehn had been exceptional at what she did, but Addison wasn't a slouch at planning. It had gone faster than even Rodrigo had expected.

"Certainly," Addison said after a beat.

"Shipwide, Lieutenant," Carlos called, and one of the men nearby nodded.

"My name is Addison Wolcott," he said in a rich voice. "Currently attached to the Rio Alliance Navy as a Commander, but I am not one of you. I am a Churquen, born on the planet Gowook far from here in what is currently referred to as Innruld Space."

Rodrigo watched him take a breath and flex all the scales around his eyes and jaw, which was a measure of emotional intensity.

"We're going to Innruld Space, you and I, to help overthrow those same Innruld, who call themselves the masters of the galaxy in much the same way that Westphalia would," Addison continued. "In doing so, we will free the forty species currently ruled by those specist bastards. We are sailing in harms' way in a Patrol Cruiser, because the journey is long, but the Innruld ships we encounter will not even be as powerful as *Dutra*, so you will be one of the mightiest battleships on the line, when it comes time to fight."

Even Rodrigo felt the emotions well up as Addison spoke. Hopefully, the man would be willing to remain in the fleet when this was done, because Rodrigo da Silva could see Addison raising his own admiral's flag one of these days.

"Your Captain is Gnashiiley," Addison said. "I am Churquen. Remahle who accompanied me and is working in logistics is Kr'mari. The Admiral is Human, like many of you. My friends back home include Yithadreph, Vaadwig, Ilount, Necherle, Tarni, Qooph, and even Atomarsk like Lt. Commander H'Brige Slani, recently of your sister ship *Recife*. We are doing this because no one species should control all the others, Innruld or Human. Ladies and gentlemen, we're going to go save the galaxy."

Addison more or less collapsed like a weak spring at that,

nodding to the inner group. The lieutenant cut the line and Rodrigo felt the emotional tide turn and surge back out of the harbor.

Wow.

Now, he just had to go live up to that sort of legend.

TWENTY-TWO

OLUCHI

OLUCHI WONDERED if he should start taking correspondence courses in whatever spare time he could scrape out of his day, to finish a degree and maybe take some law school or accounting classes. Sure as hell, he was way beyond anything he'd ever trained for, back when he was just a gigolo.

Or maybe not. That job also involved reading people and finding a way to get everyone what they wanted out of an economic exchange, on the way to a recurring or ongoing relationship.

You just had to squint and turn your head a little, and he had turned himself into a pimp. His prostitutes, however, tended to be captains of industry these days. Merchant princes.

Money and power on system scales.

But everyone really just wanted a happy ending when it was done.

The evening suffered a monsoon, so the balcony door was closed and he was seated in a chair just inside, watching the waves of squall lines pass the quad below every few minutes.

The glass of wine in his hand was getting perilously close to making him get up to finish the bottle, but he wasn't there yet.

Knocks at the door intruded.

At least they had taken to knocking. One weekend he was supposed to be off duty, Oluchi had pointedly spent two days wearing absolutely nothing. The third time someone stomped in without knocking, they had taken a hint and started behaving again.

"Come!" he yelled over his shoulder.

He heard the door open and then close a moment later.

The silence was compelling enough that Oluchi turned to look.

Middle-aged bureaucratic male. Well dressed in that fussy but plain suit they had turned into a uniform and token of their station, a sedate blue that would look like a rock in the darkness. And have about as much emotional impact.

Bureaucrats.

"I am instructed to inform you that your lawyer has arrived, Mister Pryce," the man said in a slightly disbelieving voice.

Lawyer? What in Hades name had Eha or Anya done now? Maybe Erlyn had planted a time bomb somewhere in the bureaucracy when she left?

Oluchi was unaware of any lawyer, on retainer or otherwise. A pitifully few people even knew where he was.

The man waited a long beat for an answer. Receiving none, he spoke now.

"Would you care to be conveyed to a conference room, or shall I bring her here?" he asked helpfully.

Her?

Oluchi finally managed to arrange his thoughts into something at least as organized as a pack of ducks on the good hallucinogenics.

"Here would be fine," Oluchi stammered.

"Very good, sir," the bureaucrat smiled enigmatically and withdrew, leaving Oluchi utterly gobsmacked.

This did call for more wine. He rose and surveyed the bottle, noting that it wouldn't serve two people, so he left it and pulled out one of the better red blends they had taken to delivering regularly.

Oluchi just had it uncorked when the door opened.

And he felt the rest of his world turn upside down.

Fortunately, Oluchi Pryce was an expert at keeping his opinions to himself when necessary.

Poker face, and all that.

He studied her, not asking a raft of stupid questions in a room that was no doubt being monitored in spite of promises otherwise.

How in Hades had Fernanda Flores found him? She should be on Yisan with the others. And pretending to be his Solicitor?

If he had to describe Fernanda to a stranger, he would have suggested her as on the lighter side of zaftig, carrying a few extra pounds but putting them to curvy use in a most distracting way. She could portray the matronly, grandmother type that she was at sixty-two, but she was more fun and athletic in bed than women half her age.

But then, this was a woman who had largely kept him around as an activity partner: going hiking, camping, surfing, and skiing; and not just someone to warm her bed and tell her she looked sexy naked.

Not just.

At least she was dressed for the part today.

Calf-length skirt in gray wool with pinstripes. Sensible black leather shoes with a man's heel rather than a woman's. Starched white shirt that buttoned up the front with a few frills. Double-breasted half-jacket cut wide to focus the eyes on her chest and her waist. Brown leather briefcase she must have borrowed from one of her own lawyers, to get that particular scuffed-with-age look to it.

Like most of the Humans on Yisan, she had that darker, red-brown skin tone of *America del Sur*, with straight gray-white hair shoulder length and curled under at the ends. Crows' feet around the eyes and mouth when she smiled, which was most of the time. Not a woman to dye her hair back to black. You got her as she was and liked it or you could piss off. Not quite in Eduardo's class for wealth, or Leena Hernández, who was commonly her social competition, Fernanda was still fabulously wealthy.

Oluchi just pulled out a second glass and poured one for her to go with his.

She approached with a smile like an eight-year-old pulling one over on the grownups and took the glass.

"So I'm in need of legal assistance?" Oluchi began ambiguously.

Technically, they supposedly weren't monitoring his private suite, but most of what they might have heard would be him in the shower, or him and Anya when she had free time, which wasn't all that common for reasons she had not been at liberty to discuss.

Something to do with Erlyn going off with Addison, and Anya's needing to help Erlyn's staff.

Oluchi didn't particularly appreciate the twinkle that came into Fernanda's eyes.

"Unless you've radically changed course from the man you have been for the last five years?" she chuckled and took a sip. "Probably."

Oluchi recorked the bottle and grabbed his now-full glass. He gestured her to the couch and took a moment to spin his own chair around to face back into the salon area.

Fernanda kicked off her shoes and curled her legs

sideways as she leaned on the arm of the sofa, somehow still managing to look like a lawyer, a dressed pinup girl, and maybe a reporter interviewing him, all at once.

"Technically, I'm currently indigent," Oluchi pointed out, watching her as he drank some of the red.

Fernanda grinned in a knowing, devious way.

"I'm sure we could come up with a payment plan of some sort," she offered in an innocent voice.

Oluchi hesitated. That surprised him even more than her arrival.

"That might present something of a problem," he countered.

"So I've heard," Fernanda grinned at him and licked her lips. "She must be one hell of an interesting woman, Oluchi Pryce. I look forward to meeting her sometime soon."

Okay, good. Whatever else Fernanda Flores had heard, she knew about Anya Persaud and didn't begrudge him growing up.

He just hoped Fernanda wasn't about to try seducing Anya. She might succeed. He could barely keep up with either of them. Both at once would probably just kill him.

"So what brings you to Brasilia, Fernanda?" he asked. "Besides my ongoing and possibly compounding legal and political issues?"

"You've been telling everyone that you were a representative of Eduardo Martìnez and the merchants of Yisan," she pointed out, letting her face and voice both go stubbornly innocent. "Eduardo might have been willing to take that on faith, but some of the others expressed…*concern* on the topic. I volunteered to investigate. After all, I'm still licensed to practice law in the Rio Alliance."

"I had not known that," Oluchi replied.

"It was rather a long time ago, but worth paying the fee

every three years," she laughed. "Especially now, since they couldn't argue with letting me in here."

"Have I been charged with anything?" he asked, just barely not including the key word on the end.

Yet.

"Not as of this morning," Fernanda laughed. "I'm sure it's just a matter of time, knowing you."

"Pardon me?" he said. "The only thing I've done recently is blow up a yacht, rescue an alien diplomat, seduce a spy, and negotiate trade deals to make everyone on Yisan even wealthier than they already were."

"That's what freaked Leena and the others out, Oluchi," Fernanda said, sipping her wine. "They don't understand why you were going to all that effort. But then, they didn't ever bother looking past the pretty façade. Not like some of us."

Oluchi blushed at the lascivious grin on her face. When had he turned into someone who blushed?

Anya. No. Eha.

Yes. Eha slithering into that restaurant and sitting there, next to Aileen and Lazarus, just daring any one person to walk up and introduce themselves because they had only left one empty chair.

You had to want it bad enough to walk in there alone. And fly out into the teeth of a storm to attack a yacht filled with armed kidnappers. And jump into a raging sea and let a Churquen woman wrap her panicked tail around you and squeeze because she was facing the scariest thing her kind could imagine.

Oluchi Pryce, suddenly acting like an adult.

Probably the scariest thing he had ever faced.

"All of you have been good to me," he managed. "Eduardo made it a point of putting me there with Lazarus and Grace, when Eha needed rescuing. But even before that, I made a lot of money and had inordinate fun with money from the rest of you, whether taking it at the poker table or living off your lifestyles."

"Your way of paying us all back?" she asked.

"Making it up to you," he corrected her.

"So now what?" Fernanda asked in an open-ended kind of way.

Oluchi could see the open door to his bedroom from where he sat. The implications of her words were obvious, for all the woman's subtlety. They'd been intimate any number of times over the last few years, right up until the day he left Yisan with Eha and Lazarus.

Now, he had Anya in his life. No promises, maybe, but suggestions of promises.

Possibilities.

Whatever an ex-spy and a retired gigolo might make of the second half of their lives.

Weird.

He didn't think Fernanda was the jealous type. She never had been, when some of the wealthy women of Yisan had more or less passed him around like a new recipe back on Yisan.

And Anya had apparently won a bet with Erlyn Teixeira over him, when he didn't attempt to seduce the Councilor who reminded him so much of the woman seated across the room.

Oluchi smiled at Fernanda. It was an evil, compelling smile.

He noted the hint of concern creep into her eyes.

"Licensed to practice law in a Rio Alliance court?" he asked innocently.

She hesitated before answering, as though she could see the trap door opening at her feet.

"I am," she said carefully.

"Willing to put some sweat equity into things?" he followed up even more ambiguously.

It was cute watching her suddenly take a mental step back as she tried to guess what he was about to suggest. From the look in her eyes, it would be the wrong guess. Not that he was opposed to enjoying a night of wild sex with the woman, but not if it was going to cost him Anya.

Even weirder.

But Fernanda and Leena and the others had just been rich, bored women looking for something to keep them entertained. Someone to see them as beautiful women, rather than expense accounts with tits.

A person who might just sit on the couch and listen to her bitch, because that was all a woman really needed some nights.

"What are you up to, Oluchi Pryce?" Fernanda asked in a hard, serious voice.

"Negotiating the future of Human relations with a whole host of aliens, Fernanda," he replied simply. "Who wins. Who loses. Who gets rich. I could use a little help here."

TWENTY-THREE

AILEEN

SHE WASN'T TOO sure about all this, but Aileen would do her part. Today, that involved impersonating a Director sailing a heavily-armed yacht into Gowook orbit.

Her, in charge. For real and everything, because Lazarus and the rest of the Humans were staying out of the bridge, working mostly in engineering to clean and fix things. Even Ereshkiki Nisab had been impressed with how much better the existing generators were running than they had been when the ship was captured. And life support.

And the transponders had been adjusted. And. And. And.

Aileen had made them rip out the command throne for that stupid stork of an Innruld and replace it with something her size. There had been a Yithadreph in the prior crew. Male, but not that much bigger than her.

This one actually suited her. Nothing on *Ajax* had until Thadrakho had built her a few that they had left behind.

"Coming up on the station's horizon," Kuei announced, just like she would have if Addison were coiled up here.

Eha's cone had been offset to one side with a good view,

as one did when one owned a luxury yacht more dangerous than about anything out there in this tonnage category. Human Star Spear and everything.

"Hail them and let them know we don't have any cargo to declare," Aileen said distinctly.

Cargo would require an inspection. Private yachts weren't supposed to be hauling anything important enough for the authorities to care.

"*Astral Jewel*, this is Gowook Control," a voice came over the line anyway. "We show no record of your registration."

Aileen turned to Eha and shrugged.

"I'll take this one," the Ambassador smiled. "Open the video line, please."

"*Done,*" Cormac said.

"Gowook Control, we've never landed here," Eha said simply. "The vessel is out of Batta most recently, on an extended pleasure cruise, and now I need to return and handle some family business before departing again."

The ship didn't have a big screen, but smaller ones at each station. Aileen watched a middle-aged Innruld with pretty features appear. He was dressed as a fairly high ranking civilian.

On Zhoonarrim, he might have been the governor of the station. But that was Zhoonarrim. Gowook was several dozen times richer and more populated than that dead-end system.

"Family business?" the Innruld asked impertinently. "What manner of business?"

"Tountoun family affairs," Eha replied dryly, impersonating a scion of one of the wealthiest Churquen clans with her haughty demeanor. "Inheritance and control of one of the family corporations, since you feel the need to pry, Inspector. What was your name again? No, better, I just need your badge number."

Innruld were the masters, but anybody on Gowook knew the Tountoun family of Churquens. Even Aileen had heard of them, and she'd never been to this system.

The Innruld paled. It was like watching paint fade to perfect whiteness as he assumed that she was about to call the Planetary Governor to complain.

Aileen kept her snicker internal and her face perfectly calm. Her ears didn't even come forward, although that was her forcing them to stay upright.

"That will be unnecessary, Madam Tountoun," the Inspector replied hastily. "You'll be cleared for landing. My most profuse apologies for the misunderstanding on my part."

And the line went dead.

"*Signal is terminated,*" Cormac announced unnecessarily.

Eha blew out a heavy breath as Kuei and Aileen giggled.

"Wow," Aileen finally managed. "How did you know that would work?"

"I didn't," Eha admitted. "But it works on everyone else. You just have to convince them that you will go complain to their supervisor, or better, someone at the very top of the food chain. Most of the time, they're just being bullies, unprepared to run into someone willing to challenge their supposed authority."

"And had he insisted on boarding and inspecting?" Kuei asked.

"There would have been shooting," Aileen said with a grimace. "Either at them as they approached, or after they boarded, depending on how big of a ship they might have brought over."

Eha nodded.

This had moved beyond the simple games. People were going to start getting hurt.

Soon.

TWENTY-FOUR

EHA

GOWOOK. Eha hadn't been back to her homeworld in years, mostly because she was forever working. And, if she was going to be honest with herself, she had wanted to be closer to Addison, who forever stayed clear over on that fringe of space, up against the Phraettis Nebula. The middle of nowhere, except that soon it would become a highway to Human Space.

She wasn't showing her pregnancy yet. Apparently Humans bulged in the middle as they progressed, but she would simply thicken some. Anyone but a Churquen would probably not even notice, and her people would not see anything for several more months.

It was early yet. At the same time, the little one was a reminder that the time to change the future had arrived.

Now.

Astral Jewel, the name they had given the stolen ship, was just about to land on the surface of the planet. Given her last few landings, Eha knew a twinge of anticipation, perhaps mixed with a solid dollop of rage.

But that was her. Dreamer. If anything, it was frustration

that she could not just cast a spell and make things better. That she had to work through people. Understand them. Manipulate them, even, to get them to come to her understanding of things.

But she agreed with Aileen, watching Kuei settle on the pad with a soft kiss. The time might have also come for violence.

She feared that. It was a djinn who might never willingly return to the bottle, once freed to wreak havoc and destruction. Humans found it second nature, which was even more frightening.

She would have to overcome all of that and prove that the Innruld could be defeated, rather than simply annihilated.

If she could.

"We've landed," Kuei announced unnecessarily as she started shutting things down. "I let Lazarus and the others know as well."

Eha nodded. Took a deep breath and let the air purge something in the center of her being. Fear? Disappointment?

Whatever it had been, she would consume it as fuel. Use her body as a furnace to turn raw iron into steel. Forge it into a sword for now, until she could turn it later into a plowshare, either here or on one of those secret worlds she and Addison had talked about.

The Churquen would be free. The only question at this point, at least in Eha's mind, was whether the other species could join them in that freedom.

"Eha?" Aileen asked tentatively.

"Gathering scales," she replied sheepishly. "Sorry. So much to do."

She typed a number into her system and let the local comm network route it.

The system connected and beeped twice. Eha hung up.

She dialed it again, beeped it twice more, and disconnected.

"Now we wait," she said simply.

The Humans needed to remain aft. Out of sight, so that a camera did not pick them up.

What she was doing was going to be strange enough, complicated enough. Adding the Humans to the mix would make it that much worse. At least for now.

Later, they became necessary. Either as allies, or as mercenaries that she could aim at the Innruld to destroy everything.

Eha shuddered clear to the tip of her tail.

"You okay?" Aileen asked in a quiet voice.

Eha turned to her and focused on the Yithadreph woman. Addison swore by Aileen. Lazarus had come to feel the same. Eha was learning how strong a personality Aileen Enjehn really was.

"No," Eha said honestly, looking around to include Kuei and even Cormac in the conversation. "We've all talked about rebellion. Liberation. Freedom. But we're about to slither out into the deep water looking for it and I'm a little scared."

"You?" Aileen laughed. "I'm utterly petrified. Have been for weeks. I don't know how you and Addison could do this for years."

"Really?" Eha asked. "You've seemed so calm."

"You can't see my tail shiver under these capri pants, Eha," Aileen's laugh sounded more like a sob now. "It's fine that Humans are crazy. I'm hoping you can pull a galumph out of your pocket and surprise everyone."

"Working on it," Eha replied, feeling the tension suddenly bleed out.

She shared a laugh with the others.

Eha had forgotten that the others might be just as scared as she was.

The comm chirped and interrupted before things got any stranger.

Eha took a deep, calming breath, feeling everything suddenly settle into place, like smooth scales after a good night of sleep.

She keyed the line.

"Who is this?" a female voice came across the line.

The screen remained blank, but Eha recognized her tone. Smiled broadly. She opened the video line the other direction so the woman could see her. Identify her.

"Your daughter Eha," she said simply. "We're in town and I hoped to be able to see you."

"Eha?" the woman gasped. "I didn't recognize the routing number."

"You wouldn't believe the story, even after I tell it to you a second time," she laughed. "My ship just landed in port and I would love to be able to host you for breakfast tomorrow, after I have a chance to have fresh supplies delivered. I have lots and lots of news."

The video feed came live now, showing an older Churquen woman, crinkled around the jaw and with her stripes fading down into a dull monotony of aging.

They did that. Eha wasn't looking forward to it, but she also wasn't one of those people who would dye their scales, or just stripe themselves in defiance of age. She'd spent too many years expecting to never have to face those sort of mundane futures.

The woman's eyeslits narrowed suddenly as she studied Eha.

"Yes," she said slowly, knowingly. "Yes you do, young lady."

Eha found herself blushing at the words. And the implications.

She knows.

But at the same time, she smiled in spite of all of her scales flaring outwards.

"The third hour after sunrise?" the woman asked.

"That would be lovely," Eha replied. "Mom, it's really good to see you."

"You, too, kiddo," the woman said, and then cut the line.

Eha felt a surge of tears from the emotions churning through her, but they were good ones. Happy things. Maybe enough to offset all the bad things she was going to have to do.

"Wow," Aileen muttered. "Awesome trade-craft. I never imagined an older cell contact pretending to be a parent. Great way to throw off the authorities."

Eha turned to her and giggled just a little.

"No, actually," she said. "That's my mom."

"Really?" Aileen and Kuei managed in harmony.

"It's been the family business for a long time."

TWENTY-FIVE

LAZARUS

LAZARUS UNDERSTOOD the need to remain hidden. He had that Ares pistol strapped to his hip at all times, but that was just in case someone rushed them and boarded the stolen ship, hoping for surprise. Afolayan and his crew were just as keyed up. Singh and her engineers just generally rolled their eyes at everything and kept tinkering, but they were also armed.

Prepared.

Singh and another woman had the main engine feed in the process of coming apart for cleaning and review. She and Lazarus both had ideas on how to improve it, mostly because they had both been trained on such antiquated systems when they were pups. Before moving on to the modern stuff the Rio Alliance Navy used.

But Lazarus was just an observer. So he stood off to one side, as much out of the way as he could get while Singh's team worked. Ereshkiki Nisab was working on the life support system right now, since it could be turned off except for the blower fans.

Give them two weeks on the ground, and even the

former crew might not recognize their old ship from the inside. Certainly, it didn't stink nearly as bad as it had. Couple hours on the ground and they would fully vent the old air, too. Lazarus hoped that he could buy something like orange or lemon trees to plant in pots.

Eha slithered into the engineering bay and looked at everything.

"How did it go?" he asked her, studying the woman.

She was in charge. Her mission. Her network.

He was just brute force. It was kinda nice not having to make decisions for a while.

"I made contact with the locals," Eha said enigmatically. "A Churquen representative will be joining us for breakfast tomorrow, promptly at the third hour. Cormac is placing orders for fresh food for delivery soon."

"Promptly?" Lazarus asked, catching the one word in her sentence that stood out. "You've worked with this agent before?"

Her whole body lit up, not just her eyes. He hadn't seen Eha smile like that since Addison had left.

"Promptly," she said with a huge smile. "And yes, I've known her for a long time. She's my mother."

Lazarus felt his head come up in surprise. Others listening around them had similar surprised reactions.

"Oh," he said. "You hadn't mentioned that earlier."

"I didn't know," she replied. "It's been more than three years since I've been on Gowook, and any number of things could have happened. All I had was a routing number to contact, and a set of codes to use with whoever I reached. She happened to be the one that called back."

"Good trade-craft," Lazarus nodded. "Do we want a full crew breakfast, or a small one?"

"You, me, Aileen," Eha replied. "Kuei wants to sleep in. Cormac is ambivalent. I would like Dubaku Afolayan and

Ishani Singh to join us, representing the sorts of Human expertise and scope we have brought to the table. She'll be alone, so we should fit in the wardroom comfortably."

"And we're sure she's safe?" Lazarus went ahead and asked anyway.

"We are not," Eha said after the slightest hesitation. "So we will be prepared for both violence and flight."

Lazarus nodded.

"Questions?" she asked.

"None at present," Lazarus replied.

One step forward. Or maybe one slithered wavelength.

But Lazarus was looking forward to getting home to *Ajax*, where he could dictate terms to the Innruld.

He still had a war to win with Westphalia after this was done.

TWENTY-SIX

EHA

SHE WAS NERVOUS, but what woman wouldn't be. Eha hadn't seen her mom in three years. Had only exchanged vague pleasantries by mail in between the coded messages updating the entire network about what she had been doing in her corner.

Insects gnawing at the foundation of the Innruld. Quiet revolutionaries.

Eha looked around the room and concluded that quiet was over. She would have to become an admiral, to use terminology Lazarus had taught her. A military commander in charge of strategy and entire sectors of warriors.

He had shared with her books on Human history that she found as appalling as she did mesmerizing. Guerrilla operations, which was more or less what she had been doing, but only at the lowest setting. Humans had invented entire mythologies and business degrees in how to escalate things right up to shooting wars.

And that might be what it took.

Deep breath.

Lazarus was here. Aileen as well. Grace, calm and sure.

Lucas, trying not to look like a security goon and doing a reasonable job at it. Afolayan and Singh, strangers becoming friends. The rest of the crew was awake, but staying at either end of the vessel for now. Out of the way but ready in case something bad had happened.

It had not been accidental that Kuei had landed the ship lined up with the control tower for the entire field. All she had to do was takeoff about thirty feet and elevate the bow a few degrees, and she could shatter that tower with a single shot.

Eha shivered as she wondered if Humans had infected her with their madness, or simply liberated her to envision a world where harming any Innruld didn't invite massive reprisals. She found herself sounding more and more like Addison with her internal monologues.

Hopefully that was a good thing.

The shipwide system pinged.

"A ground car just pulled up and parked in the loading bay," Kuei announced. "One Churquen visible driving."

Eha rose from her cone and gestured the others to sit back down again as they went to rise.

She wanted to do this herself.

"Churquen exiting the vehicle and scanning the ship," Kuei continued. "She can't decide if she's impressed or pissed, from the look on her face."

Eha stifled a giggle into a snort. That described her mother perfectly.

Eha exited the wardroom and moved to stand at the inner edge of the airlock. The outer door was open so that mother could get inside and out of sight.

"The woman is approaching the vessel now," Kuei maintained her commentary. "Distracted tail flicks suggest she is not at all amused and might have even recognized the type of vessel we've stolen. We might all be grounded after this."

Eha heard laughter from the room behind her. And possibly echoing from both ends of the ship.

"Entering airlock now," Kuei said. "She is alone and I am opening the inner door."

Eha watched the door move, unable to decide if it was too slow for her, or too fast.

But it opened. At the same time, the outer one closed, securing everything.

Eha felt like a teenager again, coming home late from a date to the vidshow.

Alla Dunham coiled there and studied her as the hatch finally got out of the way.

Neither woman moved for a long moment.

"Has that damned pirate at least made an honest woman out of you finally?" Alla asked, her voice tart but still humorous.

Eha found all her scales flaring. Inside her coil, that stupid tail refused to remain in place, tapping the deck noisily.

"He doesn't know yet," Eha replied, barely above a whisper. "I had to send him back in my place, so I could return to Innruld Space. But yes, he and I are finally together."

Alla uncoiled and surged forward, catching Eha by surprise with a hug that went all the way down their coils.

"Then I'm happy for you," Alla said, pressed up against her.

Alla leaned back finally and studied her closely.

"So the last news from the network was that my daughter had turned into a fugitive at Zhoonarrim," Alla said. "You disappeared without any trace, at the same time Wolcott blasted out of the station, so I presumed you left with him. What happened? And what is this ship?"

"I left with Addison, yes," Eha said, pausing to take a deep breath. "We went to Human Space, and I have been negotiating with them."

"Is this a Human ship?" Alla gasped.

"No," Eha grinned. "We hijacked it from the customs station at Onunk. But I have Human friends with me. They've been rebuilding it for us to use."

"This ship cannot take on a Security Barc, Eha," Alla said. "Let alone a pyramid. How will it help?"

"This ship is a Security Barc, Alla," Eha replied, calling her mother by her first name, just to get into the habit. "We stole it from them. There will be others, but we needed to reach the network, to activate it, so that when my Human allies are ready, we can step in and throw the Innruld down."

"Throw them down?" Alla asked. "Are you mad? How would that even be possible?"

"His name is Lazarus of Bethany, Mother," Eha said with a broad grin. "I'll let him explain it to you."

She unwound herself carefully, keeping an elbow hooked so they could slither into the wardroom together. Everyone was standing now.

Churquen could rear up on their coil, but in their normal posture every single Human in the room was taller than Eha or Alla were. Aileen looked almost like a child at the adult table, except that she wouldn't begrudge anyone else an inch of space or attitude.

Alla gasped and stopped. Shellshocked. Awed. Possibly grounding them all after this was done, to quote Kuei.

Lazarus stepped away from the table and bowed formally.

"Madam Dunham, I am Lazarus of Bethany," he said in a deep, rich voice. "The man that this original crew rescued from certain death and helped to get home. We returned to help them, and brought help of our own. Please be welcome."

Eha kept her face calm as Alla nodded slowly in return.

Eha guided her mother slowly to the head of the table, where Lazarus would be at her right and Eha at her left, with the rest spread out from there. Ereshkiki Nisab would have been the least surprising person to see here, but he preferred to tend his engines over revolution, so Alla got to meet her first Atomarsk instead.

But then, he was already fifteen centuries old, and only into middle age for his kind. What would his lifetime see?

Khyaa'sha arrived with food better suited to Humans and Churquen than the rest of the crew, but Wybert, like Ereshkiki Nisab and Kuei, had insisted that he needed to be at his station, manning the guns in case of trouble.

Eha remembered to breathe. It was her and Aileen, along with Alla, dealing with all the Humans and Atomarsk. Perhaps an appropriate metaphor, all things considered.

Alla was in shock. That much was obvious. But Eha had been expecting it. She'd had nearly a year to get used to Humans, ranging in skin tone from the deep, dark brown of Grace and Afolayan all the way up to the speckled pinks of Lazarus.

Lazarus had gone so far as to refer to Humans as space orcs, compared to the prettier or more delicate folks of Innruld Space. Once she had researched the term, Eha wasn't entirely sure the man was wrong.

But he was here to help. The Species Underground needed that.

Needed the spark that would light the fuse that would ignite the explosives that would bring down the tower that would end the Innruld domination that would free the Churquen.

It would begin in this room, over this breakfast, with her mother watching.

See, mother? I did manage something even bigger than you did.

But those words never made it to her scales, let alone her eyes.

Alla finally remembered to breathe as well. She studied the others at the table and ate mechanically, even as they ate with gusto.

Eha nodded and reached for her tea.

It begins.

TWENTY-SEVEN

LAZARUS

LAZARUS HADN'T APPRECIATED that he would be able to see a family resemblance in the two women, but he'd only ever known two Churquen: Addison and Eha. Eha was absolutely Alla's daughter.

He smiled warmly at the woman without teeth as he ate, trying to put her at ease. It was almost like that first morning aboard *Shiva Zephyr Glaive*, trying to figure out how he would survive being shipwrecked.

He turned to Aileen, seated right next to him and across from Grace, and caught the moment of sheer embarrassment passing over the Yithadreph. The ears went all the way back, along with the whiskers, and her eyes got big as she looked up at him.

Yes, she also remembered that first morning too. Ordering him to scrub her back in the shower while he had just sort of sat there in a white noise fugue.

They shared a snicker.

Alla made a querulous noise, so he turned to her.

"An inside joke, madam," he explained. "Aileen here was

the one who really rescued me. More than once. We keep facing strange new beginnings together as friends."

"I see," the woman said in a quiet voice. "Please, call me Alla. You are all Humans?"

"We are, Alla," he nodded. "The variation in skin tone and hair that you see is related to regional differences originating on our homeworld."

His own red hair starting to come in gray in places. Grace and Dubaku Afolayan's tight curls. Lucas's straight, black hair, close enough to Ishani Singh's.

"What will Humans do to Innruld Space?" she asked, leaping over any number of less interesting questions, but Eha had explained that the woman was something of a Regional Director of the Species Underground network that included everyone except the Innruld.

She would have known that Humans were a revolution brewing.

"There are two Human nations," Lazarus said delicately. "My friends and I belong to the one that believes in equality for all species. H'Brige Slani here is an Atomarsk and there are several others, like Moah and Gnashiiley. Our enemy reminds me of the Innruld, convinced that they should maintain utter Human dominance of all species encountered. Our mission here is to keep the location of Innruld Space secret from them as long as we can."

"Why is that, Lazarus of Bethany?" Alla asked.

Lazarus glanced at Eha and got a nod from her before he continued. Alla noted that with an interested smile.

"Because Human technology is so far in advance of Innruld that we could easily conquer you if we chose," Lazarus replied flatly. "That's what my friends and I are trying to prevent."

The calm way he said it probably impacted her even

harder than emotions would have. He was stating a fact, not a wish or a dream.

Alla turned to her daughter with eyeslits wide and scales flared.

"Truly?" she asked.

"Truly, Mother," Eha answered, nodding now to include everyone. "I need you to prepare for something Lazarus calls the Apocalypse."

TWENTY-EIGHT

ADDISON

AT LEAST ADDISON wasn't having to stand watches as a full crew member. Small victories when the Gnashiiley Captain had offered. And he had not insisted when politely rebuffed.

Nor had da Silva demanded, although Addison could detect a hint of something under the man's tones that would see Addison remain in uniform. Belong to the Rio Alliance Navy? Him?

Addison was not convinced. He just wanted to go back to running cargo and being his own boss, but deep in his coil he suspected that to be impossible. War with the Innruld would eventually turn into war with Westphalia. Lazarus had hoped that they could finish the one before turning to the second.

Each day that felt less and less likely.

Today, Addison was on *Dutra*'s bridge, seated off to one side and observing a proper, Human crew go through their paces. It was a Human ship, so they were jumping to an estimated spot and then spending several hours doing surveys of the surrounding stars before moving again. Nobody had particularly good maps of the region. Accurate enough for astronomy, certainly, but not to navigate against the edges of stellar gravity wells.

Shiva Zephyr Glaive could have just sailed around the mess, but he didn't suggest that too loudly. The Human drives were still so much faster than anything he had ever imagined, let alone known.

Captain Nguema, Carlos, emerged from his office and studied things.

"All well?" Carlos asked the room.

"Survey is ahead of schedule, sir," someone replied.

The bridge crew were generally the old hands, with all the new bodies mostly engineers aft working on things while the ship was at rest.

And one stowaway Churquen wondering if he'd go down in history for infamy or fame.

"How did Oliveira manage this?" Carlos asked, moving close to Addison and dropping his voice.

"Utter luck," Addison smiled at the Gnashiiley Captain. "He told me he aimed at the nebula and jumped, expecting to fly into a star somewhere along the way and be destroyed. Except that he missed."

"Too bad he didn't leave his star plots behind when he returned," Carlos mused. "Would make this a lot faster."

"Once we get into the center, it will be easier," Addison reassured him. "I know all the ways out the other side of the Nebula. It was just the Human side that nobody ever had a reason to explore, since we were happy just hiding in there and smuggling cargo around."

"Will we be too late when we arrive?" Carlos asked. "Should we cut some corners here and worry about sending a survey cruiser later for the finer bits?"

Addison shrugged.

"You're here," he offered. "You brought an admiral and a

High Councilor. And a warship. If the Navy doesn't mind losing this vessel, we could steal something in trade for those folks to return home that want to, and we'd use this like we'll use *Ajax*."

"Do you even need *Dutra*, if you can train enough crew members for *Ajax*?" Carlos asked.

"There are hundreds of colonies in Innruld Space, Carlos," Addison said. "We need to sweep them all clean of Innruld ships, but we also will need to do something about the piracy that will immediately arise when we do. You can outrun them all."

"True dat," Carlos laughed. "But my crew will remain, so maybe we'll have to steal some more ships and thin my people out across an entire battle squadron."

Addison shivered, but he understood that the man meant well. It was just the thought of a fleet challenging the Innruld.

He found himself excited at the prospect, and appalled at what he had become.

"Good thing we've brought an admiral along," Carlos continued. "Will you take command of one of the warships we steal or build?"

Addison blinked. Ah, that was what da Silva was about. Rear Admiral Wolcott, possessed of a single star on his collar?

"We have to get there first," Addison said. "I'm sure that Kuei made this run faster, but she's already done it once and had better records."

"I'm looking forward to meeting your whole crew, Addison," Carlos laughed. "They sound like amazing people."

"That they are," Addison said, noting the language the Gnashiiley Captain used.

People.

That was the thing the Innruld wouldn't grant the

species. They weren't people, they were merely citizens, with limited rights and options.

"Sir, I'm picking up a strange signal," a female announced from forward, drawing both Addison and Carlos out of their personal conversation.

"Identify," Carlos said, moving that way directly. Addison slithered in his wake.

"Reads like a nav beacon," she said in a confused voice. "But I'm not sure why there should be such a thing out here. One of yours?"

That last bit she asked looking at Addison for help.

He leaned over her shoulder and studied the waveform on her screen. Nothing at all that he recognized.

"Not mine," he announced. "Kuei or Aileen would have put it on a different frequency, and I'm not sure about those beeps. Nothing I would do."

Carlos suddenly grew quiet and serious.

"Check it against a Westphalian database," he ordered the woman. "And locate it physically. I'll need navigation coordinates."

"Bingo, we have a match, sir. Westphalia," she said, proudly, followed a moment later by her eyes growing big. "Oh, shit."

"Indeed, Lieutenant," Carlos said. "Bring the ship to alert and somebody roust the Admiral immediately. All hands stand by for combat operations."

Addison took a long slither to his left, into a space currently out of the way as people started to move. He'd watched enough training videos to understand that certain people on the bridge were about to be replaced by others and everyone would be buttoning down and possibly getting into soft suits against a hull breach.

He had nothing he could wear, nor could Remahle, back with the cargo crew and engineers, learning Human technology, but while the Kr'mari could shelter in whatever room he was in, Addison needed to stay up here. He'd faced Westphalia once. Or at least watched Lazarus and Wybert do it. And he had fought pirates.

But if Westphalia had already come through here, they must have a pretty good idea where Innruld Space was, and just needed to find a safe corridor, much as *Dutra* had been doing.

"Any ship signals?" Carlos called loudly over the noise of bodies moving and sirens awakening.

"Negative," the signals woman replied. "Nav beacon only at present. Should I hard ping?"

"Affirmative!" Carlos yelled back. "Find out if anyone is here. Nav, prepare a jump to safety, just in case. Fusilier, unlock and stand by."

Nav beacon. To Addison, that sounded like something you left for future vessels, to make it easier for them. Like perhaps *Dutra* was already behind in the race and needed to do something.

"Carlos," Addison said to get the man's attention.

"What?" the Gnashiiley Captain snapped.

"I suspect that they are already gone," Addison said. "Ahead of us."

"Meaning?"

"Maybe we'll need to start taking risks after all," Addison replied.

Carlos nodded, so Addison called up a nav screen and began studying everything around him, flipping the map end for end, as though he was sitting in the middle of the nebula looking outwards toward Human Space.

Yes. It was risky, but that might be a path to the system where they'd originally found *Ajax*, and later left *Shiva Zephyr Glaive*.

Addison didn't know what he'd find when he got there, but hopefully not a Westphalian GunWall.

He took a breath and waited for the noise around him to subside.

"No vessels in range," the woman called. "I have coordinates on the beacon."

"Show me," Addison called.

A dot appeared on his screen a moment later.

Addison understood. This system was right at the edge of the Nebula. A hollow spot in its face, if you will, dimpled a little with clouds and young stars around them like a cone.

Addison knew which way the Westphalia force probably went, because they had no reason to take risky actions here. Through the corridor on the right, then loop around and up. It wasn't fast, but it would get you to the far side soon enough.

To Innruld Space.

Addison added that as a plot on his board and looked at the smaller space on the bottom left. It was riskier, and had nothing at all to speak for it, except that it led to the pocket in the middle where *Ajax* had landed.

He wondered if Westphalia was trying to get there, and just taking a careful stroll.

Carlos was standing close when Addison looked up.

Addison dialed the map back to a much larger scale, and added a red star for the system he wanted.

"I'm guessing they went blue," Addison said. "You would have as well, at least on this first series of jumps."

"Agreed," Carlos said. "The star is *Ajax*?"

"Where *Ajax* originally came out," Addison agreed. "And where we left my ship to come to Rio if I read this correctly. The red path is riskier from here, but I think we can punch through and get ahead of them. Maybe."

Admiral da Silva appeared. Erlyn Teixeira was on his heels as they entered.

Rather than ask stupid questions, they moved close and watched.

"Permission to get crazy, Admiral?" Carlos asked, showing the plot screen Addison had worked out.

"Westphalian force ahead of us?" da Silva asked.

Addison and Carlos both nodded.

"Do it," the Admiral said.

"Con, I have a new plot!" Carlos yelled and transmitted it to the man's screen. "Refine that and prepare to jump. But first, let's destroy that beacon."

Addison watched as the ship started accelerating.

It had suddenly become a race, and Westphalia was winning.

TWENTY-NINE

RODRIGO

ADMIRAL DA SILVA had become a flag officer again, after a few weeks as a semi-important guest aboard *Dutra* on one of her regular long-range scouting missions. Once that beacon had been blown up, he had grabbed Carlos and Addison, and Councilor Teixeira, and retired to a quiet office. Big enough for the four of them. Small enough to keep secrets.

The day had that sort of feeling to it.

He studied the outsider here, still chuckling a little in his mind that Councilor Teixeira was the odd woman out. Rodrigo's mind accepted Addison as another officer under his command. At least for now.

"So let's go over it again," Rodrigo said, mostly for Teixeira's sake.

She hadn't been in all the military planning meetings he'd had to stay awake through.

"The line of escape from *Ajax*'s first battle was known by Westphalia," Addison said. "That gets them somewhere, but we can presume that a spy let them know that Innruld Space was huge, so that leaves off being inside the Phraettis Nebula itself."

"Agreed," Carlos said. "I'd be looking to get to the far side of the nebula and then just plant myself and listen for radio signals."

"Would that work?" the Councilor asked. "Aren't we talking hundreds of light-years of distance?"

"We are," Addison agreed. "But remember that Innruld Space has been static for thousands. If your tools are sensitive enough, and have enough processing power, they can pick up signals, especially as ships exiting the nebula over there would land somewhere and verify everything before jumping again."

"I thought you could just sail around things?" she asked.

"You can, but the nebula is a mess," Addison explained. "You end up passing extremely close to a lot of weird gravity anomalies in there, and your sensors usually need recalibration."

"Should we be chasing them, then?" Rodrigo asked. "Kill their beacons as they lay them? Presumably someone with the right passwords could get the beacon to tell an invasion force which way to go."

"I still think that they're headed to the place where *Ajax* was at," Addison said. "That makes the most sense, if you don't know the area, and there is a big galaxy over here, once you get through."

"Agreed," Carlos spoke up. "I'd want to find the space where *Ajax* landed originally, and then start scouting outwards from there. Especially if they have no idea where the closest inhabited worlds are located."

"Do we know what we might be facing?" Teixeira asked.

"Maybe," Rodrigo said. "Westphalia's fleet is all about their GunWall. Small ships operating in teams of five, with four escorts and a command ship."

"ScoutWall?" Carlos asked.

"Most likely," Rodrigo agreed.

Teixeira and Addison were confused.

"Take a Phalanx," he explained. "Their main escort ship with a Star Spear and eight Powerbolts. The ScoutWall pulls four of the Powerbolts for a better sensor array and reduces the crew to increase sailing range. Their Scout Archer is built like a CommandWall variant, also pulling the small guns and cramming in enough Flag facilities to control a whole Patrol. Wverything is dedicated to scouting. They make excellent electronic warfare ships when you encounter them, but that's rare."

"Can a Patrol Cruiser engage a ScoutWall, Admiral?" Teixeira asked simply.

Addison leaned in to hear his answer.

"Maybe," Rodrigo said. "Straight on? No, but if we come up on them from behind, they might be surprised enough that we can hammer them. The gun shield only protects you from the front, after all. Pity we don't have *Ajax* with us. That ship would go through them like shit through a goose."

"Should we break off and circle back to pick up their path?" Carlos asked.

Rodrigo turned to Addison.

The Churquen Commander paused for a second, eyes unfocused.

"I'm only guessing," Addison said. "Assuming the path they took, but *Ajax* originally threaded a needle perfectly to get where Lazarus did. I've studied the paths and he shouldn't have been able to do it, so maybe only a ship fresh out of drydock could have pulled that off, from what I've learned about your drive systems. I think they'd want a better path. Safer. But once they got there, you have any of seven corridors out to Innruld Space. For us, the question was which system you wanted to approach after a smuggling run. I normally hit Dormell or Zhoonarrim because they represented outlying systems that didn't have a lot of traffic and were on my regular circuit, but an Innruld Squadron could just as easily hit Aceanx, Krahua, or Gorm. All they would have to do is sail close enough to a habitable star and listen. Eventually they find someone to talk to. And conquer."

"Assuming they move slowly, plotting stellar motion well enough for future fleets, how long to get to where *Ajax* was?" da Silva asked. "Does that system even have a name?"

"It does not," Addison smiled at him. "Nobody lives there and every ship and cell called it something different, in case they got penetrated. Way better to confuse spies."

Rodrigo chuckled at that, seeing more of the real Addison who had been lurking behind the officer pressed into service.

"Time?"

"If we don't hit anything, we ought to get there in a few days," Addison said, turning to Carlos.

"My team will surprise you," Carlos laughed. "They're looking at this as a challenge, since a Vaadwig Pilot already did it. Don't want her to show them up, you know."

Rodrigo joined the laughter, but it still felt hollow to him.

Westphalia had stolen a march on him. On them.

Maybe on the Innruld.

What would happen when they knew where to fly their fleets to?

THIRTY

AILEEN

SHE HAD NEVER SET out to be a spy. Or a Command Officer, for that matter. Aileen had just wanted to solve her three-dimensional puzzles and fly cargo for a living.

They were a long ways from that ever happening again.

As it was, she'd assigned Lazarus to handle Cargomaster duties on *Astral Jewel* while she was gone, because he insisted that he couldn't leave the ship under any circumstances. It wasn't quite that bad, but the damned stork with the good fingernails could be almost as stubborn as her when he wanted to be.

Wasn't worth the fight right now.

Alla Dunham had come and gone. Met the Humans and H'Brige and been about as utterly freaked out as Aileen had expected.

Now Aileen and Eha had to go talk to some people about rebellion.

Gowook was a nice world. They had landed in the southern hemisphere, in a medium-sized coastal metroplex. The populace was largely Churquen for the planet as a whole, but the city of Ersop was much more cosmopolitan, to the point that she didn't particularly stand out as she and Eha walked and slithered along a simple concrete sidewalk in a nicer neighborhood.

Aileen wasn't used to real weather, but at least it wasn't raining right now, although the forecast said it was coming.

Listening to weather forecasts was just weird, and Aileen was trying not to obsess over it. Nothing ever changed on a station or a ship.

The ground floors around them were all shops or entrances to larger stores that might take up a whole city block. Everything was towers around her, four to ten stories tall, with residential in most of them and a few that were primarily dedicated to office space, for those businesses that actually needed everyone in the same room for meetings or something.

Not too many Yithadreph around, but more than say Qooph or Vaadwig, which was another reason she'd drawn this duty.

You couldn't stand out as a spy. Or whatever the hell Aileen had gotten herself into now.

"You're doing fine," Eha offered as they approached one building, slipping through a door that led to the residential lifts, between a bodega and a scale salon.

Churquen worlds could be strange places.

"Feeling weird," Aileen admitted.

She reached inside her jacket and touched the weapon Lazarus had insisted she carry. He called it a Manticore light laspistol. Probably was to a Human. Her hand could barely get around the grip, and the weight of the thing made her feel like she was walking off-balance.

"We're almost there," Eha reassured her.

Into the lobby, waiting for a lift. Aileen found herself studying the space. Nobody around. White tile floors that hadn't been cleaned this year. Gray tiles to about shoulder high that might also be white if someone went at them with the right chemicals and enough patience. Wood above tiles that looked old enough to have dried completely out and started to rot.

If there was a better metaphor for Innruld Space, Aileen wasn't sure she'd heard it so far.

A Tarni emerged when the lift doors opened, eyeing the two of them askance as he skittered sideways and around, heading for the back entrance. No words were exchanged, just looks, but the best Aileen could say to describe the man was furtive.

The whole city had that feel, come to think of it. Had it gotten worse in the last year, or was it always like this on the ground? In space, everyone was a little more something. Welcoming? Polite?

If the Innruld pissed off the merchants, they would just stop calling at a station. If enough of the merchants left, the populace had to go elsewhere to find jobs.

Maybe the masters of the galaxy didn't have to pretend to be nice, down here on the ground?

Eha pressed a button and the doors closed. Up and then they were on the fifth floor, exiting and turning down a hallway.

If the lobby had been bad, this corridor was worse. Aileen could smell the despair. It tasted like rancid cooking grease that should have been recycled a month ago, mixed with a harsh ammonia or something that was used to clean around here.

The floor had originally been gray tile, but someone had covered it over with a laminate at some point. An orange and yellow flower design probably intended to brighten things up. Except that foot traffic had worn paths in the plastic, back down to the tile, leaving curled edges. The walls might have been painted white at some point, but Aileen assumed that enough beings just breathing could bring it down to that faded grungy color that might be a good mix of brown and gray and looked like a mustardy mold that had died of depression and *ennui* along the way.

Aileen didn't think she'd made a noise, but Eha glanced back over a shoulder.

"Sorry," Aileen said.

"I understand," Eha replied. "This is a poorer sector, but that's on purpose."

On purpose? Why the hell would the Innruld intentionally depress the homeworld of one of the largest, most productive species in Innruld Space?

Oh, right. Revolution. Better to keep them poor and shackled. Less time to make political demands if just putting food on the table was hard enough.

They turned a corner and went down a back hallway. Eha stopped and knocked on a particular door and they waited.

Aileen hadn't seen anyone else since she entered the lift.

Just entropy.

Eha knocked again on the door. Nothing complicated or fancy. Couple of raps to get the attention of those people inside and let them know that they had visitors.

It was probably just Aileen's imagination that she heard guns come out of holsters and safeties turn off.

Sound of someone approaching the door. Peephole got dark, light, and then dark again. She wondered if someone had stood to the side and covered it with a thumb against someone else shooting.

The corridor, hells the whole building, had that sort of a feel to it.

Long pause, like they were being inspected, in spite of being expected.

Or maybe because of it. High-stakes poker, as Oluchi would have called it.

Bolts started clearing on the other side of the door. More than even this neighborhood suggested necessary.

Finally, it opened and a Kreeghal woman eyed them, then stepped back into the hallway beyond, gesturing them to pass. Eha led. Aileen gave the Kreeghal some stinkeye, but that was just professional courtesy. She was feeling rude and unruly right now.

The inside was a world apart from the other idea of the apartment's hatch. Door. Whatever.

Someone had painted in here. Bright pastels that immediately lifted her spirits and suggested hope. There were ever plants in pots, which was weird, but helped. Like walking through a jungle.

They emerged into a clearing. Or a living room. Something. Less plants. More space. People in chairs and on a couch.

Alla Dunham was there. The Kreeghal stood by the door. Deeper in were two new Churquen males and…son of a bitch?

Aileen was going for the pistol when Alla flared up and waved both hands to distract her.

"He's with us," Alla said loud enough to get her attention.

Him? Really? An Innruld?

Aileen studied the man. Growled, but stopped short of doing anything, realizing that there was a reason the Kreeghal woman had followed so close. Aileen could smell her perfume and glanced over.

Yup, about to get tackled.

She gave the woman a sickly smile and blew out a breath.

Aileen turned back to the Innruld and studied him. Tall, lean, pretty. Middle-aged, give or take. Perfect blond hair long and pulled back into a tail but not a braid.

Well-enough dressed, but she wasn't used to Innruld not

in uniform. You found a few as merchants on stations, but usually as overseers and assholes in charge.

This one was dressed like an office worker. Did Innruld have companies without any other species employed? Weird.

He had flinched at her reaction. He flinched now at her disdain, but gave her a weak, understanding smile.

"Aileen Enjehn, this is Turkan Volan," Alla introduced them. "He's with us."

Aileen wanted to inquire if everyone here was insane, but that much was obvious. They were all rebels, after all.

She nodded to the man, specifically not grumbling at him.

"Turkan, this is Eha, my daughter," Alla continued.

Eha had the grace to slither close enough touch the man. Wasn't a coil, but they rarely did that with bipeds. Too easy to knock them over.

"Sit," Alla commanded, so Aileen did.

The nameless Kreeghal woman sat close enough to tackle her if Aileen got feisty, not that she blamed anyone.

Eha surprised the hells out of her by turning this way and smiling.

"I don't understand anything military, so Aileen, could you explain to everyone what you've done?" Eha asked.

Aileen fought hard and managed to keep her ears from going back flat. She drew another breath and held it for a second.

"So we found a new sentient species in deep space," Aileen said. "Long story with a lot of details and mixed outcomes of adventures, but they've sent help into Innruld Space. Not much, but they didn't need to send much."

"Why is that, Aileen?" Alla asked carefully.

She already knew the truth, so this was for the benefit of the others.

"Human technological sophistication is greater than Innruld," Aileen replied simply. "Significantly."

"How significantly?" Turkan asked, his pale face whiter now.

"The main Human warship could blow up Zhoonarrim Station without breaking a sweat," Aileen said. "It's hidden in deep space right now, and we stole a small Security Barc, modified it as camouflage, and are flying around in it so we could get here to talk to you folks."

She expected the Innruld to pass out from the news. That was about the only point farther down the scale he could go. Instead, he flushed, almost with excitement.

Really? An Innruld?

Turkan turned to Alla with an excited smile.

"You could actually do it?" he asked her.

"We believe so," Alla nodded. "But there is a problem."

"Which one?" Turkan laughed. "I have notebooks of potential problems we've tried to plan for."

"The Humans hold it in their hands to break the Innruld," Alla said. "Shatter their power so suddenly and so completely that Innruld Space as we know it collapses into chaos overnight."

Yup, back to pale.

He turned those pretty eyes on Aileen now, and she couldn't help but smile at him: mouth, whiskers, AND ears.

"You said destroy Zhoonarrim Station?" he asked. "That wasn't a euphemism?"

"That's one shot with the big gun," Aileen said happily. "Chop the damned thing in half like a diamond cutter."

There. That was the color of Innruld White she had been expecting.

He even gulped, which made her whole week better.

"I appreciate that you and I might have slightly different opinions on the topic," he began, searching carefully for the words. "What about the innocents aboard a station like that? Not everyone there will be deserving of such a cruel fate, however much my cousins might be."

"That's why we stole a smaller ship," Aileen said. "So we could sail around and not have to kill every Security Barc and Pyramid we met. Most of the Pyramids don't have any guiltless aboard."

"Granted," he nodded.

Then he surprised her and turned to the other two Churquen. They sat close together like brothers, but didn't have any sort of match to their scale patterns, so she didn't think they were related. Best friends?

"Do we launch the Ark?" he asked them.

"We think it might be premature at this moment," Eha suddenly spoke up, which was good because Aileen was lost. "But we think that the extended organization needs to be prepared for such an outcome."

"Ark?" Aileen asked anyway.

Turkan fixed her with those bluish-gold orbs.

"In that moment when the Innruld lose control, there is a plan to collect a set of vessels with enough colonists to start a new civilization outside Innruld control," he said in a hard tone. "I and my kind are not welcome on those ships, but part of my contribution to the cause has been access to the databanks necessary to plan."

Aileen touched Eha's hand to get her attention.

"Vilga's Stand?" she asked.

Nobody else in the room would appreciate the meaning.

Eha nodded and Aileen felt her ears go back in spite of anything she could do to stop them.

"Does Lazarus know?" Aileen pressed.

"Not in so many words," Eha said. "But conceptually he is aware of that as an option. It is a known system, inhabitable, with allies we believe we can trust over the long term. The alternative was any of a number of other systems that people like Addison have surveyed over the decades, but they are less valuable, because each represents sailing into the darkness and rebuilding our entire civilization almost from scratch."

Aileen blew out another heavy breath, wondering if this was going to become a habit.

"What about Westphalia?" Aileen asked. "Out of the frying pan and into the fire?"

"Risk," Alla said. "All things bring risk, but the rewards might be worth it. Certainly the Species would fight Westphalia even more savagely than the Innruld, having had a taste of freedom."

"Shit." Aileen didn't seem to have any better way to sum it up.

"Indeed," Eha smiled.

The next question she wanted to ask was derailed by the Kreeghal woman suddenly standing.

"We have a potential alert," she announced in a hard, quiet voice. "Innruld security vehicles are pouring out of several stations around the city. They appear to be centralizing here."

Aileen studied the woman and realized that those three eyes were staring hard at her. And she had a small comm piece tucked into one of those pointy ears to listen.

The Kreeghal wasn't quite as tall as Aileen, but outweighed her by a bunch. Long arms and short leg on a biped. Hair like a Human but all over her body, rather than something like fur.s

Tough. Hard. Aileen would settle for shooting the woman, rather than trying to wrestle. She'd lose that match quickly.

"Are we betrayed?" Alla asked the room.

Aileen noted a lot of panic on the faces around her. Less

so on Eha and the Kreeghal, but she seemed to be the only one taking it in stride.

But then, in the back of her mind, she'd been waiting for the other shoe to drop.

"How soon until they get here?" Aileen snapped at the Kreeghal. She didn't even know the woman's name, but now was not the time, especially if some of them ended up in jail by sunset.

"Two minutes," she replied.

"Not long enough to do more than walk out the front door into their hands," Aileen mused.

She reached into her jacket and grabbed the Manticore with one hand and her comm with the other.

Aileen keyed the system as people around her started to stand and mill around. Galumphs waiting for the rancher.

"*Astral Jewel*," a deep, careful voice replied.

Lazarus, rather than Kuei. That was good.

"I have an emergency," she said simply. "Three minutes to catastrophe."

"Get to the roof," Lazarus said.

"Acknowledged," Aileen said, turning to Eha and smiling as she pocketed the comm. "You heard the man."

"What's going on?" Turkan demanded.

"I've got help coming," Aileen said, nodding the Kreeghal woman to get to the door and open it so they could flee.

"What can your friends do against a security patrol?" Turkan challenged.

Aileen smiled up at the even-taller-stork. She laughed.

"Give you a taste of Human violence," Aileen said.

The others didn't understand what that meant. Not even Eha, although she'd been with them at Zhoonarrim when Lazarus lifted a damned filing cabinet and put it into place with only his back muscles.

Aileen waited for the rest to get out ahead of her. Now

was not the time for someone to panic and try to cut a deal with the Innruld. This smelled like a setup, but she didn't know enough to cast aspersions.

But she also knew Lazarus was about to move heaven and earth.

Ersop was just going to be the first to taste his wrath.

THIRTY-ONE
LAZARUS

LAZARUS THREW himself into the command chair of *Astral Jewel*. It fit Aileen, but he had also put in everything necessary to adjust it back to his size. Kuei and Cormac had been waiting, but he hadn't told them what they were waiting for.

Wybert had understood, and was aft in the control station for the upgraded gun.

"Bring everything to power for atmospheric flight," Lazarus called out. "Fusilier, unlock your weapons and stand by."

"All systems live," Wybert replied immediately.

A year ago, the man had panicked and blasted Lazarus's pincke into salvage because he'd never actually fired the guns on *Shiva Zephyr Glaive* at another vessel.

Today, he was going to become the sort of warrior that got to mate with queens.

"*We are prepared for free flight*," Cormac announced as Kuei continued playing what Lazarus could only compare to piano concertos on her boards.

Lazarus smiled grimly.

"Kuei, we're already aligned with the tower," Lazarus said. "Get us enough elevation to destroy it, keeping the bow up and the tail down so any blow-through doesn't hit anything beyond."

He expected her to look back at him in horror, but she'd flown for Addison against pirates and for Lazarus against Westphalia.

"Lifting now," she replied instead.

"I have targeting lock," Wybert's birdlike voice came over the intercom.

"Engage and destroy," Lazarus replied.

His screens already showed the tower that controlled all traffic over a fairly large section of sky. The entire terminal control area for Ersop, which tended to be big.

The Star Spear was a magnificent upgrade from the main beam that the ship had come with. But the same could be said for many Human weapons. And Innruld concrete wasn't any stronger than the Human stuff.

The control tower exploded like someone had planted a bomb at the tip.

"Grace and Lucas to the bridge," Lazarus announced before cutting the intercom. "Kuei, you have the coordinates?"

"Already plotted and moving!" she yelled back over a shoulder and started south into the city.

Now it became a race against time. Aileen hadn't argued about getting to the roof, so whatever it was, it was happening on the ground.

But it was also more than she felt comfortable dealing with. That was why she had called him and invoked the most serious call for help from the ones they had prepared.

"*There are two security aircraft over downtown,*" Cormac announced. "*Currently orbiting above the building that is our destination.*"

Aileen had said *catastrophe*. That meant Innruld arriving to arrest her and blow the entire mission to hell.

Worse, capture her and Eha, plus whoever else.

"Wybert, shoot down any security aircraft in range," Lazarus called, knowing that a lot of people were going to die, not all of then Innruld. *In range* meant a lot, even in atmosphere. Those two, plus whoever else lifted.

"Stand by," Wybert called. "Engaging."

Grace and Lucas arrived together, already armed, with Lucas also wearing his usual field armor.

Grace was deadly enough without it.

"Situation?" Lucas asked.

"Aileen has a problem big enough that she called in the cavalry," Lazarus said. "We're going to unleash hell on the Innruld of Ersop and rescue her and Eha and whoever else needs it."

"All security aircraft have been destroyed," Wybert announced over the intercom. "Standing by for new targets to engage."

Lazarus had been following him on a screen. The first two plus another one way over at the far edge of town, but Aileen had said it was desperate.

The Innruld were getting the hammer today.

Grace nodded in a compact way. Lucas grimaced. They'd been briefed, but nobody had been prepared for what might happen, other than it might come to this.

Apparently, it had.

"Grace, you're in charge aft," Lazarus smiled at her. "I told Aileen to get to the roof of the building they were in, because she said they were about to be surrounded."

"Do you want us shooting police?" she asked in a detached voice.

"Not unless you have to," Lazarus said. "Most of them won't be Innruld. Just folks making a living. I presume half of them are thugs with truncheons, but we can't stop to ask. Return fire without mercy, but I'd prefer not to have a mass casualty incident today. We've already done a lot of damage to the city just getting here. It will get worse before we escape."

She smiled at him now, warming.

They still had their moments where they didn't agree, but she was helping temper some of his bloodymindedness.

"Let's go, Lucas," she said, dragging the marine in her wake.

Lazarus studied the scans. The shock would start wearing off in a few minutes and the Innruld authorities would be able to respond. Right now, they were frozen in place and the people controlling the flight patterns above Ersop weren't answering the comm anymore.

Soon, someone would realize why, and place a call to orbit for help. Nothing on the ground right now could stand up to a Star Spear, after all.

A targeting lock on one of his screens showed the building that was their destination. Lazarus presumed that was Wybert making sure who not to shoot at if things got hectic. The Fusilier had grown into a dangerous job.

Now to rescue his friends.

THIRTY-TWO

EHA

EHA LED them to the roof, getting to the lift before the police could arrive to intercept them. She didn't know what had gone wrong, but she was beginning to suspect a serious leak in the organization. This was the second time a surprise police raid had been centered on her, going back to Zhoonarrim station.

Eha didn't think her mother had betrayed them, and the Innruld was so nervous right now that she wondered if he would faint. But the others were strangers. That had been the whole point of this meeting, to start things expanding.

"Move," she snapped at the Innruld as he stumbled out of the lift.

Eha turned to her mother.

"Get them organized," she ordered the woman, inwardly a little surprised at herself.

But then, they had no idea what was coming.

Eha did. But she'd been seated in front of a desk while a Human held a gun to her head. Lazarus had stomped open the door and Xiuying had killed almost everyone in the room, with Grace firing the final shot that ended Strav Ardna.

From the look on Aileen's face, she remembered that night, too.

"What happens now?" Eha asked as Alla got everyone to cover where they could not be immediately seen from the lift entrance.

Before Aileen could answer, a flash of light lit the sky above them followed a moment later by an explosion.

They watched something fall out of the sky on fire, but Eha couldn't tell what the various pieces might have been before.

"Lazarus is coming," Aileen said with a grim smile. "Do we trust these people?"

Eha shrugged. For anyone to be in this meeting, they had to have been investigated and thoroughly vetted.

"Maybe someone on the outside set us up?" Eha asked. "If it was a trap, I would have expected them to already be here. This feels like someone saw something or a neighbor called the cops."

"We'll find out soon enough," Aileen replied. "You should get to cover, since I'm hopefully the only one armed."

"Hopefully?" Eha asked.

"Anyone bringing a gun besides me expected trouble, Eha," Aileen said. "Keep that in mind."

Eha nodded sagely and moved to where her mother was ducked behind an air vent.

"What was that?" Alla asked, gesturing in the direction of the flyer that was impacting the ground below. Or maybe bouncing off the side of a building.

"The Humans are coming to rescue us," Eha replied. "I told you about the yacht and the storm."

"You did, but I don't think I believed you," Alla said, her eyes showing a little too much white right now.

Eha looked around at the others. Aileen was grimly pointing her pistol at the lift door, apparently less worried about the police immediately finding them since there were no onlookers above them.

The rest of the conspirators were all in sight of one another, with nobody acting particularly suspicious right now. But as Aileen pointed out, everyone needed to be checked for secret weapons or a radio comm before she would trust them.

"What will the Humans do?" Alla asked.

"I don't know," Eha said. "But I trust that it will involve extravagant violence because that's what Lazarus does when someone threatens his friends."

"Are we his friends?" Alla asked.

"Aileen and I are," Eha turned to her mother with a stern gaze. "How far are you willing to trust the others?"

"They've all been with us for a long time," Alla said. "But that doesn't mean anything right now. This might be a thing big enough to blow a deep cover for."

"Just so you understand where I'm coming from," Eha said. "Do we rescue everyone off planet, or just you and drop the rest somewhere safe?"

"Turkan needs to come with us," Alla said. "They'll torture him to death if they even suspected that he was a sympathizer. The rest can be turned loose for now, with instructions to activate all the cells."

"All the cells, Mother?" Eha asked, surprised that the woman would take that step.

"As you said, Daughter," Alla laughed. "This is the revolution."

Movement across the street, up on the seventh floor of an adjacent tower, caught Eha's eye and she realized that someone was standing in their open window, talking on the comm and gesturing at them.

"Aileen!" Eha yelled, pointing the Yithadreph woman to the person presumably talking to the police.

Aileen nodded and thankfully didn't fire a shot that direction.

"Company coming!" the Yithadreph warrior did yell as the door opened and a pair of officers stepped out.

A Churquen and a Kdari, both wearing Innruld blue.

Aileen shot them both, getting the Kdari first.

Eha shuddered at the implications.

Yes, the revolution had just begun.

THIRTY-THREE

GRACE

GRACE STOOD in the airlock door and contemplated the piece of equipment that Ishani Singh and her folks had added. A winch on the end of a telescoping crane, with a cargo net on the end that would be able to lift just about anybody to safety.

What did it say that those engineers had presumed trouble and gone ahead and solved the problems as they'd identified them?

Still, it was going to save her a lot of effort today. Maybe some lives.

They were approaching the building. Grace had attached a safety line around her waist and leaned out to watch. She had a headset so she could talk to Lucas, standing next to her and also attached, over the noise of the ship hovering. They could also talk to Kuei up on the bridge.

As for Lazarus? He simply trusted her to handle it.

That put a smile on her face.

"Down twenty feet and rotate another ten degrees right," Grace said into her microphone.

She could see the target, but there were two buildings

around them that were taller, so the space in which to operate was compact.

The turn brought the rest of the roof into view.

A bolt impacted in the hull not far away with a sizzling snap. Handheld, so it wouldn't penetrate, but somebody on the ground was taking exception to her being here.

Grace saw a stairwell door open and two Kreeghal in blue uniforms, carrying rifles, bounded into sight.

Aileen shot one of them, but the other got to cover.

Grace turned to Lucas.

"I need suppressing fire," she pointed at the rest of the roof.

Lucas nodded and opened up with his own pistol. Not a great crossfire, but Lucas knew what he was doing.

Grace put a shot into the other Kreeghal when the being popped up to shoot and dropped him. As Lazarus was wont to say: *War is an unkind mistress.* While these weren't soldiers, they were the enemy.

Grace put a foot into the harness net and started the winch.

"Lucas, put me on the roof and then stand by to bring people aboard as we clear the place," she ordered.

"Yes, ma'am," he replied, putting one hand on the controls while the other continued popping off shots at anything in blue.

Grace let the winch drop her forty feet to the roof. The ship was hovering over one edge, but she had enough clearance.

And the rain had started. Not bad, but a penetrating mist that got in everywhere with cold fingers. She'd need a hot shower later.

"Lucas!" she yelled, waving a hand.

He cut the winch and Grace hooked it for now over a

light fixture as she took an inventory of the people trapped on the roof.

One Kreeghal, four Churquen, an Innruld(!?!), and Aileen.

Grace fished into a thigh pouch and pulled out a boarding grenade. Innruld issue, stolen along with the ship. She'd brought two with her.

"Lucas, covering fire," she called into her mic and then counted to three as the marine above her opened up, before she rushed the stairwell entrance.

Aileen had been murder up here all by herself. There were six officers down or badly wounded, but they also didn't have any cover emerging from the lift. As a result, they had stayed back to the stairwell instead.

Grace fired a few shots into the well-lit doorway as a way of saying hello, and then hurled the grenade as hard and low as she could, bouncing it off the far wall and letting it roll down the stairs.

She ducked to one side as a flash of light preceded a whoomph of air rushing out.

For fun, she counted to ten and flipped the second one in. These were designed to blind and stun, rather than throwing metal shards everywhere, but it would be miserable to be trapped in a stairwell with one.

Another hard thump.

She closed the door and dragged a body against it from this side to hold it in place for now.

"Cargomaster, do your thing!" Grace yelled at Aileen, but the woman was already in motion.

Everyone got chivied towards the net. Churquen fit well, since they could coil themselves around the gaps to hold on. The Kreeghal woman and the Innruld male got into the middle and Aileen climbed up on the outside.

"Lucas, pull us in!" Grace yelled when Aileen nodded that she was ready.

Around them, the rain was starting to get harder, but the ship was a giant umbrella as they started in the air.

Grace was opposite Aileen, both of them aimed back where the police might yet appear, but Grace figured that she'd put the fear of an alien god in their lives for now.

Overhead, one of the ship's guns opened fire at something. A moment later, an explosion rebounded off the faces of nearby buildings, but she couldn't see what Lazarus was firing at. Except that it would be Wybert at the guns.

She shivered in spite of herself, thinking about the Ilount and what he had done previously with ship's guns.

The winch got everyone up and Lucas retracted the crane into the airlock. It was crowded, but they were safe for now. Grace triggered the outer hatch as soon as she was clear and then made sure she hadn't lost her headset.

"Bridge, we're aboard," she said, maybe a little louder than she intended, but this wasn't a quiet theft or assassination.

"All hands, hang on," Kuei's voice came back.

The ship pitched and slanted for a moment, before the grav systems could adjust.

"Next stop, orbit," Kuei said.

"Negative on orbit," Aileen cut into the circuit. "We need to move to a spot at the edge of town close to a subway station where we can deposit people. Then we run the gauntlet."

"Acknowledged, Aileen," Lazarus said. "Good job everyone."

Grace smiled as she watched four Churquen untangle themselves from what looked like a polite orgy with two bipeds trapped in the middle.

They were safe, for now, but Grace knew that things were going to change.

She had never been to war. That roof, however, had been a battle ground.

There would be more of them.

THIRTY-FOUR

LAZARUS

LAZARUS NOTED THE SCANNERS. Clear skies in every direction as everybody had landed hard and fast when *Astral Jewel* started shooting.

The War of Liberation had come to Gowook.

The ship was headed to the edge of town at a calm pace barely faster than a ground vehicle, rather than tearing madly around and scorching the sky. With the control tower at the space field annihilated, it would be some time before the Innruld authorities even figured out what was going on.

"Cormac, locate all the police stations," Lazarus said simply. "On my number two screen, please."

"*Stand by.*"

Normally, the NavCrawler had an emotional voice, but he had retreated into something flat today. Not that Lazarus blamed him. His current crew were generally civilians impressed into service, not people who had chosen to become warriors. Not like him.

And Wybert.

Aileen came bounding into the bridge.

"What's the news?" he asked.

Lazarus figured there was a spy somewhere, but either an amateur, or someone who had broken cover at the last minute. He'd let Grace interview everyone they brought aboard to see.

It wouldn't even be torture, because the woman had been trained as a geisha on top of everything else. Lazarus was willing to bet a lot of money that she could identify lies, even told by aliens, just by listening to the tone of their voices.

"We're taking Alla and the Innruld with us," Aileen replied, coming to rest next to him in what was technically her command seat. She made no effort to get him to move, but again, he wasn't surprised. "The others we will let off on the edge of town so they can vanish back into the mass of citizens."

Lazarus studied her for a moment and then opened the comm.

"Grace, could you vet everyone for me real quick?" he asked. "Before we drop them?"

She would understand the term. The others might as well, but this was Grace he was talking about.

Amazing, frightening, sexy woman.

"Understood, Lazarus," she replied in an even tone.

"Alla and Eha, would it aid the cause to commit acts of unbridled terrorism against the police stations around Ersop?" he asked over the line.

There was a murmur of several voices talking in a low tone back there before Alla Dunham replied.

"Actually, Turkan suggests the Hall of Records building, off Government Square," the woman said. "Most of their records and data systems are located there and it would seriously disable their global abilities to lose that."

"Cormac?" Lazarus asked.

"*Identified,*" the little NavCrawler replied in a much more Human voice. "*On your screen now.*"

Lazarus had wondered how squeamish a robot might be about so ruthlessly taking sentient life, but not now. Perhaps he had his own issues with the robots and bureaucrats that blowing up their building might cover?

"Thank you, Cormac," Lazarus said. "Wybert, stand by to destroy that building."

"Already locked in, Director," Wybert chirped over the line.

"Fire at will, Fusilier," Lazarus ordered.

The stolen Security Barc had the main gun upgraded to a Rio Star Spear, but it also had six smaller turrets on the corners and flanks, in order to engage pirates. All of them opened up now, pouring fire into a squat, pyramid-looking building downtown. Maybe a ziggurat, since the sides stepped every few levels.

The architecture did not protect it, but it was just stone, and Wybert was apparently focused on a task of blatant destruction. After about three salvos, it collapsed inwards, fire taking hold and sending black plumes of smoke into the air that *Astral Jewel* flew through.

Lazarus smiled grimly.

The War had indeed begun.

THIRTY-FIVE

EHA

EHA WATCHED the group move quickly away from the ship, separating into individuals all going away to escape whatever was about to happen here in Ersop.

Astral Jewel lifted off from the middle of the park where they had landed as Grace closed up the outer hatch.

Eha noted that the woman was relaxed now. Grace rarely gave any sense of inner turmoil, but today the smile seemed genuine.

That was good, considering what Eha had just witnessed.

She looked around at her mother, Turkan, and Lucas.

"Would you have really been able to uncover a spy, just talking to them?" Eha asked the Human woman.

Grace smiled at her. It was disconcerting.

"The Kreeghal woman is firmly committed to the cause," Grace replied. "Turkan here has the most insecurities, but he understands that he's already past the point where he will be executed for what he's done if they ever catch him. The two Churquen men are hiding a secret, but it is not a threat to the cause."

"What?" Alla demanded. "What are those two up to? Everyone has been checked time and again."

"They're in love and have pair-bonded," Grace said evenly. "Cultural mores frown on such a thing among the Churquen males, as I understand them, although the Innruld probably foster such things."

"Foster?" Eha asked. "Why would they do that?"

"Fewer Churquen breeding," Grace said. "Among Humans, it is generally accepted that twelve to fifteen percent of any given population have nonbinary tendencies. In the ancient times, that was a sin and a crime. What are the numbers for Churquen?"

Eha had to stop and think. She didn't honestly know, so she turned to Alla for help.

"Perhaps three percent?" Alla offered. "As you said, rare. But it would mark them as rebels against the power structure. It's just that in this case, the powers they are fighting also probably include their entire families."

Eha noted that Turkan hadn't moved, but he was also hemmed in effectively in the airlock by Grace and Lucas. It did not appear to be accidental, either.

She stared up at the Innruld. This was the first friendly one she had ever met, and Grace seemed to accept him. But then, Eha had heard stories about Lazarus against a group of drunk Innruld, all young adults in a Species dive bar they probably should have avoided. Lazarus considered Grace an order of magnitude more dangerous than he was.

She let the tip of her tail shiver.

"I presume it will blow your cover to disappear," Eha said to the gangly biped. "What are the implications?"

He was tall. They all were. She could have reared back on her coil to look him in the face, but it wasn't necessary here. He felt hunched in on himself until he was barely bigger than her.

"Nothing, I think," he squirmed his face some in the way that bipeds without scales could do. He turned to Alla. "She has all the information I was able to smuggle out, and I've not seen her plans after that. Compartmentalization works in our favor here."

"Alla?" Eha asked her mother.

"Did you really blow up the space field control tower?" Alla asked.

"Yes," Eha said simply. It frightened her how casually she could discuss and plan violence, but even she had come to understand that the Innruld would never give way willingly. The Humans had done that to her. Or perhaps opened her eyes. "It was a contingency well down the list of options, but Aileen invoked the worst-case-scenario, so the Humans reacted accordingly."

"With the Hall of Records blown up as well, it will be chaos around here for many days," Alla said. "I need to send a message on the comm to several listeners before we get out of the atmosphere. Since this ship is already in rebellion, it will not blow my cover any more than disappearing will. The teams will get into motion."

"And?" Eha prompted her.

"And they will load into as many transports as happen to be local and available," Alla said. "With supplies already stockpiled for them here and in other places. With luck, there should be enough people to start a new colony without Innruld interference. Once they gather, they will vote on which of the targeted colony worlds they will head to. One small part of the revolution will have begun."

Eha studied her mother closely. Then the Innruld traitor. Finally the two Humans.

"We need to talk to Lazarus," she announced, exiting the airlock finally and turning forward. "All of you come with me."

She ended up leading the weird collection of people forward to where Aileen and Lazarus were on the bridge with Cormac and Kuei.

"Alla needs to send an activation signal to several cells to take advantage of the chaos," Eha said as every head and camera turned her direction.

Lazarus surprised her by immediately turning his console screen around to face them. "Here."

Alla slid close enough to her that they touched tips, tails, and hips. Eha almost put her arm around the older woman as a comfort, then went ahead and did it anyway, unsure who was comforting the other.

This was her mother. And Alla would be a grandmother soon. A whole new generation of rebels to rear. Or perhaps raise free.

Eha could barely remember her own father. He had disappeared when she was very young, swept up in a random Innruld net and vanished into a prison where he had eventually died of some disease. The Innruld did not put much effort into prisons for anyone else, except to keep them in and crush their spirits.

Alla looked up at Lazarus, then turned her way and returned the hug.

"It is done," Alla said.

"You know where they will assemble, correct?" Eha asked.

"I do," Alla replied. "Were you planning to rendezvous with them there? Escort them?"

"No," Eha smiled. "Well, yes, but not how you were thinking."

"Oh?"

"Lazarus, they will assemble a convoy of old freighters and yachts," she turned to the rebel himself. The man who had died and been reborn in the cause of liberty. "There is a list of potential colonies they would make for after that, where they would live rough and primitive lives while they built up an industrial base capable of starting civilization over."

"Okay," he said warily, as if he already knew where she was going with this conversation and just waiting for her to speak.

He might know. The man was brilliant at times, and just amazingly smart others.

"With your permission, I would like to lead them to Vilga's Stand," Eha announced. "Settle them there."

It was insightful that he didn't argue with her. But then, he had to have known why Addison had picked that system to explore.

"I cannot possibly give you that permission," he replied with a wary smile. "I don't speak for the Rio Alliance government, nor the corporations that originally seeded those worlds."

"Understood," Eha said. "But *Ajax* can clear the way. And it puts a colony heavy on Churquen and Yithadreph in a place where the Rio Alliance High Council can see what our technology level is. How little of a threat we present. And it is two whole worlds, so they cannot begrudge a group of refugees some space. Our intent would not be to take both, but to settle there on small claims where we could live free."

She took a breath to commit herself.

"And join the Alliance."

"Join the Rio Alliance?" Alla echoed the words. "Daughter, is that safe?"

She turned to her mother, still tangled with the woman.

"It is safer than the darkness, Alla Dunham," she replied in a hard voice, but Eha Dunham was the Species Ambassador to the Humans. That had to mean something. "The Alliance means well and I believe they will rise to occasion. Westphalia would just be a trade of masters for us, but the few Moah and Gnashiiley we bring with us will meet their distant cousins, and vice versa. That will bridge many divides."

They turned to study Lazarus now, both of them.

He had shifted his weight in the chair and was scratching at his chin with one hand. Apparently it was a Human thing when one was deep in thought.

Then he smiled.

"At the end of the day, I'm already in rebellion against my own commanders," he laughed. "If they're going to Court Martial me over this, I might as well make sure I cover as many bases as I can."

"Thank you," Eha said.

"Liberation, Eha," he replied warmly. "Kuei, Cormac, get us to orbit while avoiding anybody who wants to stop us, and then plot the fastest course you can to *Ajax*. We'll come back for *Shiva Zephyr Glaive* later."

Eha smiled as everyone got behind her idea.

It would be the biggest gamble of her life, in a career that had already seen some amazing and stupid things.

But it was the right thing to do.

THIRTY-SIX
OLUCHI

OLUCHI FOUND it utterly empowering to be seated on this side of a long conference table with Anya on his right and Fernanda on his left. Across from them, the eight remaining members of the High Council, minus Erlyn Teixeira who was apparently off in space with Addison and Remahle, visiting Innruld Space to see things with her own eyes.

It was an afternoon session, so he'd brought a pair of bottles of red with him and let the Councilors subsist on water, coffee, and lemonade. Anya and Fernanda had appreciated the effort.

He was directly across from Roald Cavalcanti, with two big ring binders between them, each about six inches tall and representing the months of work he and Eha had put in with those self-important bozos over there.

Oluchi could appreciate a republican form of government as probably the most effective, but it still grated on his nerves some days. These Councilors were empowered to take actions as a whole for the betterment of the Rio Alliance. Sure, there were larger, representative bodies, with two Senators per planet and a number of lesser politicians based on enumeration of a census, but all the power resided in the executive across from him.

The treaties they negotiated here would simply be put to an up or down vote later.

Cavalcanti was feeling his oats this morning, as well.

"Madam Flores," he addressed her with a stern voice. "In the past, we the Council have been willing to accept Pryce as a deputy for Eha Dunham and the Species Underground, understanding that without the coordinates of Innruld Space, all players assume that Yisan will likely be on one of the main trade routes connecting to Brasilia. Are you speaking for the Yisan government now?"

Oluchi smiled the same way he might when he completed an inside straight flush on the last card. Hard and mostly contained in his eyes, where a player as good as Eduardo might just go ahead and fold immediately.

Cavalcanti wasn't that good a player.

"That is correct," Fernanda replied coyly. "While the Rio Alliance does not maintain formal diplomatic relations with Yisan, it is the expectation of the leading men and women of the planet that the time has come to change that. To more openly ally ourselves with your government."

"Will you give up Westphalia?" Cavalcanti asked.

Oluchi watched the tides swirl through the eight remaining Councilors. Juan Almeida, Aatther Jamill, and the Gnashiiley Councilor Pascia Nkali representing the Humanist Bloc, evenly matched against Mara Terson, the Moah Councilor Whrlaxu C'Vorloo, and the Atomarsk Councilor Ch'ani Zen as the Alliance Bloc, leaving Cavalcanti and Ruby Martins holding the balance of decision-making, with the understanding that tie votes would be possible without Erlyn Teixeira present.

Right now, the possibility of wider trade and the need to upgrade the Species technologically suggested factories everywhere suddenly having whole new markets to expand into.

As Eduardo liked to remind people: Money talks and bullshit sits on the curb grumbling.

"We do not maintain formal relations with Westphalia, either, Chairman Cavalcanti," Fernanda reminded the man. "All hulls landing at Yisan are welcome, regardless of political origin, as long as they maintain strict neutrality while in our system. That goes all the way down to the crews of ships. Any infraction with political overtones generally gets a ship banned for a period of time up to and occasionally including the heat death of the universe."

Oluchi watched the swirl of emotion harden a little as her words got processed.

Then that lovely, dangerous woman dropped the other shoe.

"That being said, however," she continued in a harder voice, "we are not making any diplomatic advances towards Earth to improve our relations with them at this time. If and when they choose to send ambassadors to Yisan, we will hear their proposals and decide, but I will remind everyone here that the lifeblood of Yisan is trade. Goods coming and going. If we charge a lesser tax on transfers between hulls that is sufficient to offset the cost of freightage, that is an issue of taxation your worlds should take up on their own."

"So not much will change?" Ruby Martins asked now.

"That depends on the proposals you might make, Councilor," Fernanda volleyed back at the woman. "I am deputized to speak for the major players. They own the government of Yisan in fee simple, when you get right down to it."

"How far might you go?" Councilor Nkali asked.

The Gnashiiley had dark fur, almost the same

brown/black of the Humans around here, offset with a white beard wider than normal. And sharp eyes.

Fernanda smiled at all of them, including turning to him and Anya, before she spoke.

"If the price was right, we're even willing to discuss joining the Rio Alliance, ladies and gentlemen," she said.

Oluchi heard the raw outburst of noise from across the table and tasted the flavor of it. He leaned back with his glass in hand, certain that Cavalcanti would be a little while getting everyone to shut up again.

News like that would get out. You couldn't contain it.

But it sure as hell would alter all calculations. If he was correct in his assumptions of stellar cartography, Yisan and those worlds around it joining the Alliance would establish one hell of a tall fence across any paths Westphalia was interested in building into Innruld Space.

They could still send war fleets if they chose, but the logistics got strained in a hurry if you couldn't call on Yisan or its neighbors for food replenishment or repairs. Or had to risk pirates from Yisan falling on any bases you might build as way stations.

Anya's hand found his under the table and squeezed, so she had seen the same thing, most likely. He turned to her and smiled.

Cavalcanti finally banged his informal gavel hard enough to get everyone to shut up, at the cost of breaking the wooden handle in two. Probably should have brought a hammer instead.

From the look in the man's eyes, he was planning to next time.

"Order is restored," he said in a quieter voice than the previous yelling. "Ambassador Flores, thank you for that most interesting bit of news. You will understand that the

Council needs to recess now to private meetings before we are prepared to engage in more formal negotiations?"

"I do," Fernanda smiled innocently at the Council.

"I declare this meeting in recess." Cavalcanti used his fist as a gavel.

Immediately, all of the High Council rose and filed silently out the door, where they would, no doubt, find a sound-proofed chamber to scream at each other in private.

Decorum, after all, must be maintained.

Oluchi was just sad that Teixeira was going to miss all the fun. She and Fernanda were so alike in that way.

He finished his glass and rose as well, grabbing the remaining bottle and slipping it into the bag he used to carry heavy documents around.

He took each woman by the hand with a smile as he slipped the messenger bag's strap over his shoulder.

"Let's chat back in my suite," he said.

Both smiled. Both nodded. Both remained silent until they weren't immediately surrounded by witnesses.

The game had just gotten insane.

THIRTY-SEVEN

ADDISON

ADDISON HAD STOPPED REFUSING, however politely the requests were phrased, and starting standing bridge watches like another one of Carlos's officers. He understood that most of what he was doing was reminding the various crew members that he encountered that there were many more aliens out there to meet. Setting an example for future generations, as it were.

He was on *Dutra*'s bridge as they surveyed nearby space today.

"Sir, I think we have it," the navigator said, turning her head in his direction.

Addison usually coiled behind the captain's seat. He slithered around it now and approached the woman.

"Show me," he said.

"Working from your notes, this looks like the place, Commander," she said.

Addison watched her spin the map in three dimensions. Suddenly, he recognized the gap she was pointing at.

Had they done it? He'd thought that they still had two

days of jumping and listening to find it, but maybe the barrier was thinner here?

"That's it," he said, pointing a long, scaled finger over her shoulder and rotating the view back and up a little bit. "This star here? That was where we found Lazarus and where he had parked *Ajax* the first time."

"And where you left *Shiva Zephyr Glaive*, sir?" she asked with bright eyes.

"Indeed," he agreed. "Call the Captain and ask him to come to the bridge, Lieutenant. And good job."

Addison returned to the side of the main station and coiled. Carlos emerged from his office almost immediately, so he hadn't been having a nap or anything.

"We've found it?" he asked.

"Confidence is high," Addison replied, falling back into those training videos he had been watching for the last year.

"One hop or two?" Carlos queried.

"You feeling dangerous or precise?" Addison fired back.

"Nav, can you get us there in one long jump, assuming a short one when we figure out what the neighborhood looks like?" Carlos called to the room now.

"Affirmative, Captain," the woman navigator said. "Commander Wolcott's notes get more and more detailed, the deeper we get into the nebula."

"Very good," Carlos said. "Someone roust the admiral's lazy ass and let Councilor Teixeira know we're about to make a terminal jump. Oh, and all hands to battle stations."

Addison had been expecting that. Both parts. Carlos ran a loose ship, but he also had the respect of his crew and treated them well. You could joke about admirals when people were friendly.

And Rodrigo da Silva wasn't nearly the hard case that Pedro Santos was.

But now, they were about to leap into a system where

they were expecting a Westphalian squadron to appear. Whether they were already there or not remained to be seen, but from here on in, things would get a lot more dangerous.

Addison moved to a spot next to the sensors officer and coiled. He had the most expertise about the ships they were likely to encounter here, as well as the stars once the ship got through to the next layer, since the system coming up was a smuggler's haven much of the time.

Anybody but Westphalia would be complete strangers to the rest of the crew, but Addison knew how to contact them and hopefully not cause them all to flee like mad.

He needed the smugglers. Needed their contacts.

Because he had brought the war with him and they were in a race against time now.

THIRTY-EIGHT

LAZARUS

LAZARUS RETURNED to the captain's cabin after dinner and more or less collapsed into a chair. Grace had been a step behind him through the door and stood there for a moment, watching him, before she climbed into his lap and curled up like a cat he had once known.

"I won't ask if you are okay," she murmured. "I know better. What's wrong?"

Lazarus started with surprise, but then remembered that he was dealing with Grace Savidge. Geisha. Dancer. Assassin.

Woman.

Perceptive barely aimed the conversation in the right direction.

"Nerves, I think," he replied.

"You?"

The notion seemed to surprise her, but here in the cabin they shared, in the life they were carving out, he could be free to talk.

They were just words. Sometimes he had to meander through them for a while before he found the right order. Or something.

"*Pancho* Oliveira turned the bow into the storm and sailed off to die," he reminded her. "He failed and washed up on an unmarked island he thought was deserted. But he was wrong."

"He was indeed wrong." Grace leaned in and kissed him on the cheek before settling her forehead against his ear.

"Then he brought these strange islanders back to civilization with him, having bizarre and violent adventures, Odysseus-like along the way," he continued. "Except that in order to do the right thing, he had to rebel against his own people. Now, he's about to take it upon himself to hijack a future colony world and install those aliens there as refugees."

"You'll be a hero," Grace murmured in his ear.

"To some," Lazarus agreed. "A villain to others. A fool to many."

"Second thoughts?" she asked.

"Second guessing myself is a near-constant vocation these days," he turned to smile at her. And kiss her. He needed that reassurance. "I'm doing the right thing, but there are times when the cost I'm going to have to pay frightens me even more than just flying *Ajax* into a star originally."

"Court Martial and stripped of your rank and pension?" she queried.

"That's the best outcome I can see," he sighed finally. "Throw in a stretch of prison time for good measure and the Rio Alliance deciding to evict Alla's people and force them to flee back into the darkness, where they end up on one of the worlds they had originally planned, followed maybe by a wider war against the Innruld that ends up with Rio and Westphalia making species-cause against the aliens."

"They wouldn't do that," she tried to reassure him.

"They aren't supposed to," Lazarus corrected the woman. His arms finally came up and wrapped around her now, as if he could draw heat and strength from her. "But each of us only guesses at what we'll do until that moment when death is on the line. All I have right now is hope."

"But it wears thin," she said.

"It wears thin," he agreed. "I have to keep a brave, commanding face on at all times for the others, because both fear and bravery are contagious. Crews get infected by their commander. You know me better than they do, and can see when I'm dragging. Like now."

"So what do you need?" Grace leaned back to study him.

Lazarus thought about it, but had no answer. Chasing that squirrel around in his mind had been almost a constant thing over the last several days as they ran to grab *Ajax*. The return trip to where the convoy would meet would be relatively quick, so he knew he could rendezvous with them.

That was when the crazy parts would start.

He turned and studied her, almost close enough to bump noses.

For all the weeks they had shared a cabin and been lovers, there had always been some level of reserve keeping him back a little. He'd known it, but not how to bridge it. She hadn't pushed, perhaps understanding that it was his problem to solve.

"You," he finally said simply, watching her eyes grow big for a moment. "I always thought I was the strongest person I knew, but I know four women just on this ship that put me to shame."

"Oh?" she asked, her voice taking on a little bit of a teasing tone now.

"You, Aileen, Alla, and Eha," he ticked them off in his mind.

She leaned in and kissed him warmly. It felt good.

Lazarus felt some of the ball of ice in his belly start to melt as she did. He let her heat warm him.

"As a reminder," she said after a time of necking had passed, "you might be stuck with me now."

"I can think of much worse fates," he grinned. "But not any better ones."

"Think you might survive all this?" Grace grinned back.

"I might even want to," he said. "If I've got your strength backing me."

Grace kissed him and then leaned back and laughed.

"What?" he asked.

"Of course, Aileen will still need her back scritched in the shower occasionally," Grace observed.

"True," Lazarus noted. "Maybe we can find her a Yithadreph boyfriend in the convoy when they arrive. They will need the assistance of an expert cargomaster, so she'll had to spend time around complete strangers teaching them the difference between their ass and a hole in the ground."

She laughed.

"So we should turn into matchmakers?" Grace asked.

"I want everyone else to be as happy as you make me," he said, finally understanding what had brought him down tonight.

Fear of losing her. Failure that put him in prison but where she escaped back to Yisan and he never saw her again. Or maybe she simply got tired of him and went home.

She slid off his lap and held out a hand to pull him to his feet.

"Let's go cuddle," she smiled. "I can see I need to remind you why you keep me around."

"And vice versa," he said, rising and embracing the woman.

Hopefully, it wasn't going to be a last meal for the condemned.

THIRTY-NINE

ADDISON

THE STARS on the screen felt like home in ways Addison hadn't expected. It was like a weight being lifted off his tail.

"We've arrived, sir," the woman lieutenant announced unnecessarily, turning to him with a smile on her face.

Maybe his good humor was infectious. Looking around, most of the faces he could see were smiling.

"So this is where it all began?" Admiral da Silva asked, standing next to Carlos, with Councilor Teixeira on the other side.

Addison uncoiled from his space next to the sensors officer and turned to them.

"It is," he nodded. "We were here doing a hand-off with another ship when we got a signal out of the blue that turned out to be Lazarus in his pincke. After we nearly blew him up accidentally, we rescued the man and hauled him out of the nebula back to Dormell, where the adventures really began."

"So where do we go from here?" Teixeira asked. "And did we beat the supposed Westphalian force?"

Supposed because nobody had seen them yet, but hopefully they had arrived first. *Dutra* had been cutting corners for speed, and a five ship squadron would be that much slower as every vessel had to rendezvous after a long jump and get organized.

"Sensors?" Carlos called out.

"Negative on other signals, Captain," the woman replied.

Addison nodded. It felt right. You had to thread several needles to get here, although this was the most obvious spot for Westphalia to arrive, once they back-calculated Lazarus's flight path to escape them. Safer to take a longer circuit, though.

Even if that let a sneaky Churquen steal a slither on you.

Addison reached out over the woman's shoulder and touched a spot on her screen to indicate an orbital path.

"That ice giant is where we left the ship when we headed to Rio space," he said. "It will look like a tiny moon in this orbit until you get extremely close, because we shut down everything and transferred all the water and oxygen to *Ajax*."

"I'm looking forward to seeing your ship, Addison," Carlos said with a smile. "Never seen one that was asymmetric before. Nav, lay in a single jump and execute. Sensors, be awake when we get there."

"I'm always amazed at Human designs," Addison replied with a matching grin. "There is no reason at all to make something streamlined if you don't plan on landing on a planetary surface. Symmetry is just silly either way."

Dutra was a long, flattened cylinder with a tapered chisel at one end and a flare for engines at the other, even though it didn't use thrusters to move around. Just riding on grav fields, and doing it in silly symmetry.

"Stand by for jump," the navigator called. "And through."

Addison turned back to the other screen and studied as she pinged all the moons and junk in orbit. This was a messy system. Lazarus had managed to find a gravitationally-stable point, but it had taken a lot of processing power to prove it.

And even then it was only going to have lasted for another decade or so before it degraded, at which point it would have been the luck of the draw whether *Ajax* spiraled into the ice giant's atmosphere or just got ejected into deep space, never to be found again.

Shiva Zephyr Glaive was much smaller than *Ajax*, so it had much longer.

But he was really looking forward to standing on his own bridge again.

And maybe showing it off to the others. They needed to really understand how primitive Innruld Space was.

Addison smiled at the memory of Lazarus learning about trans-space. Knocked that poor biped right on his ass. Maybe he should do the same to the other Humans on a short flight.

"Tentative contact identified," the sensors officer called in an unsure voice that had Addison over one shoulder and Carlos the other even before the echoes had faded.

Addison stared at the screen and muttered a mild profanity he had learned from Aileen years ago. He turned to Carlos and noted the gloating grin on the Gnashiiley's face.

"Ya know, Addison, that doesn't look like *Shiva Zephyr Glaive*," he said. "Why would they park *Ajax* here and take your ship, if they were intent on doing violence?"

Addison shrugged all the way to the tip of his tail.

"I'll ask Eha and Lazarus when we find them," he replied. "For now, I'll assume they wanted to sneak someplace where they could land and talk to the locals. Maybe foment some revolution or something."

Carlos just smiled. Like maybe he'd already done the math and wanted to tease Addison some. Addison had just automatically expected Lazarus to sail someplace like Dormell or Zhoonarrim and issue demands.

He kept forgetting that Eha would be calling the shots, most likely.

Addison turned to Rodrigo da Silva.

"With your permission, sir, I'll take a crew of engineers and some folks from the bridge, and head over," he said. "If and when Westphalia gets here, we have them far out-gunned now. And we can leave a note here for Lazarus and Eha when they get back. Or we can wait here for a week or so and see if they return."

"I've read the reports," Councilor Teixeira spoke up suddenly. "How well would *Dutra* stand up against a Security Barc in combat?"

"The heaviest ones would be hard pressed to win a battle against this ship," Addison turned to the Human woman. "A pyramid would be too dangerous to engage, but *Ajax* could annihilate one of those with Kirov's Lance. I presume you wish to go to Dormell or Aceanx and scout them?"

"Possibly even open communications, Commander," she said. "My writ from the High Council is extremely vague and open to interpretations, once we got someplace where we could acquire actionable intelligence."

This did not sound like the politician he'd been talking to before. Erlyn Teixeira came across with those same vibes as Eha did.

Fortunately, he was used to dealing with that woman, as well.

"As long as you understand the implications to the Species Underground, madam," Addison retorted carefully.

"Relax, Addison," Teixeira suddenly smiled. "I have to be able to honestly tell those shits from the Humanist Bloc that we didn't just sail up and open fire. I take you and Eha at your word, but sensor logs will go a long ways towards making our case to the general public."

"Especially if they open fire on us without provocation?" da Silva chimed in.

"Most definitely then," she agreed. "Not that I would

ever suggest you provoke them into shooting first, just to prove my point."

"Can they hurt us?" Carlos asked, a little apprehensive.

"Keep them nose on square, like you had Kirov's Lance to aim," Addison said. "Reinforce everything forward. Power the engines themselves at low draw with the generators running flat out. Have a spare escape hop programmed that you can activate if they try to surround you. Even *Dutra* should be fine for a couple of minutes if they open up with everything they had."

"Would *Ajax* even notice?" da Silva asked.

"Not until a Pyramid maneuvered over to try us," Addison smiled. "And they have the speed and flexibility of small moons in open space."

"In that case, Commander, you will take command of *Ajax* for the time being," da Silva ordered in a formal voice. "I will transfer my flag over there, freeing Carlos to be annoying to his own crew, and Councilor Teixeira will join us. Carlos, you get to go back to flying escort for a while."

"Not really surprised, Admiral," the Gnashiiley grinned. "But I would like a chance to test *Dutra* against a Security Barc, if they get frisky."

"Captain," Addison interrupted, "if they identify us as rebels or Humans, I am reasonably confident that they'll get frisky. The Innruld stand atop a rotted column of wood, constantly working to shore it up. My job is to provide a stiff breeze or a hurricane blow, because I want to topple those bastards."

"Trust me, Commander," Carlos said with a hard smile. "So do I."

"Alert!" the woman on sensors suddenly called out in a hard voice. "Blueshift detected. Unknown vessel, presumably enemy. Check that. Multiple signals inbound. Westphalian flags evident on transponders. Enemy squadron has arrived."

Addison cursed. He'd gotten here ahead of them, and then perhaps led the enemy right to *Ajax*, when they never would have found the ship otherwise.

He looked up and caught Carlos's sympathetic nod.

"All hands to battle stations," Carlos called. "Prepare to engage the enemy."

FORTY

LAZARUS

LAZARUS LAUGHED to himself as they prepared to drop out of trans-space. He was indeed going to need more crew members, just for all the ships he had already stolen, to say nothing of the ones he still planned to go after. He hadn't asked who was going to join him on *Ajax*, Cormac or Kuei. That would be their call and both were more than qualified to sit that duty with him.

The civilians were in their cabins or the wardroom until the ship got closer. Nothing would be visible for at least another hour, as they located *Ajax* in orbit and sailed in close. Wybert was aft in Engineering, last Lazarus checked, learning the finer points of gun maintenance from the men and women he commanded.

Aileen had only grumbled a little about being promoted to command *Astral Jewel*, but he didn't have Addison around, and her rank was greater than anybody else. Even if she did threaten to tickle him until he surrendered.

"What's so funny?" Aileen asked, standing next to him as he sat in the command chair that would be hers in a few hours.

"Probably have to teach Lucas or Ishani how you like your back scratched in the shower," he grinned.

Oh, the grumbly pout on her face. Lazarus felt his grin expand until it almost hurt.

"I am not putting a uniform on," she noted drily.

True to her point, today she was wearing faded mustard capris and a deep maroon doublet that laced up the front.

"It's okay, my little pirate babe," he teased her some more, just because he wouldn't be able to when they were commanding separate warships.

Aileen really was his oldest friend in the world. *Pancho* might have older ones, a very few, but he wasn't *Pancho* anymore.

He had become Lazarus of Bethany instead, and the galaxy would come to know that name shortly.

If he had to do it as a pirate king, so be it.

She grumbled, but it was with a grin on her face. She'd known Remahle longer, and the entire crew of *Shiva Zephyr Glaive*, but he understood that she had kept all of them at a level of reserve similar to how Lazarus dealt with people.

So he and Grace would need to go through all the Yithadreph men and disqualify any that weren't going to measure up to Aileen's standards. Or theirs.

"Coming up on emergence," Kuei announced generally, glancing back over a shoulder to give them a moue of disappointment at the two of them.

What did it say about the galaxy when Kuei Akeley was the one acting like a grownup?

"Yes, Mother," Aileen snarked back at her.

Everyone chuckled. Even a century-old NavCrawler.

Out the big window everything was a pearlescent gray shot through with those incredible streaks of blue.

Trans-space.

On the one hand, Lazarus looked forward to sailing in a

vessel so fast that it fell through a hole in space and emerged. On the other, how much more beautiful was it to fly in here?

The engineer he portrayed when he wasn't being a pirate had spent a lot of time thinking about ways to make a trans-space drive run faster, mixing in Rio tech. It wouldn't be as fast in a straight line, but at the same time, Rio Alliance ships had to land, look around, and then jump frequently, in order to get around gravitational dimples in hyperspace that you didn't even want to fly too close to.

Over the distance between Brasilia and Zhoonarrim, that might make a faster trans-space ship a better fit, especially going through the nebula with all those twists and turns.

Akeley's Passage, as Lazarus intended to enter it into all the sailing directions.

Immortality for a dork of a Vaadwig. And another of his friends.

"Three. Two. One. Emerged," Kuei counted them down.

Trans-space vanished into reality, the black firmament of night lit by billions of stars, most of them obscured by the vast clouds of dust and gas representing a stellar nursery. "Oh, shit! What's that?"

Lazarus was in motion before his brain caught up with his hands. Seatbelt pulled tight, where it had been loose and comfortable before. All screens snapped around and locked in.

Brain and heart racing.

"*Six signals detected in orbit of the ice giant*," Cormac explained with the patience of an electronic being. "*Ajax is not responding, but I have the Rio Alliance Patrol Cruiser* Dutra *moving to engage with a strange squadron of GunWall ships.*"

"Describe strange, Cormac," Lazarus ordered, even as his hand slapped the big red button on his screen and alarms started sounding. "All hands to battle stations. Fusilier to your guns."

Aileen slipped to a station close by, strapping herself in and powering everything up.

"*The vessels all scan at a lower power output than the ones we engaged previously, Captain,*" Cormac replied enigmatically.

"Show me," Lazarus ordered, looking at his screen as they came up.

He blew out a big breath of relief a moment later.

"ScoutWall," he announced.

"Meaning?" Kuei asked in turn.

"Fewer guns, less generators, smaller crews, more stores for long-range exploration," Lazarus said. "A Patrol Cruiser couldn't stand against a GunWall, even with our help. ScoutWall is a smaller, weaker force."

"Aren't they still tougher, stronger, and meaner than *Astral Jewel*?" Aileen asked, studying an echo of his screen.

"Yes, but they don't know that," Lazarus said. "We have a Star Spear, same as they do. Plus, those gun shields only work in one direction. Kuei, make sure to keep them between us and *Dutra* until they start to run away from us. Cormac, identify us to *Dutra*."

"You're nuts," the Vaadwig woman snapped under her breath.

"You knew that," he fired back. "But we're the Rio Alliance Navy, Lt. Commander Akeley, and our job right now is protecting Innruld Space from Westphalia. That means we have to do crazy right now."

"Should we try to get to *Ajax*?" Aileen asked. "That would end things real quick."

"No way in hell a pincke would be safe in all that mess," Lazarus replied. "You'd be a sitting duck for whatever gunner wanted to take pot shots at you as you waited to dock. No, we have to chase them off right now, and then maybe chase them wherever they go so they can't get a message back to Earth with the right coordinates."

"*We are being hailed,*" Cormac announced. "*Admiral Rodrigo da Silva's compliments to* Pancho, *along with High Councilor Erlyn Teixeira, Captain Carlos Nguema, and Commander Addison Wolcott.*"

Aileen cheered loudest, but everyone joined her.

"He did it!" she yelled. Lazarus assumed that she opened a com back to where Eha and Alla were sharing a bunk. "Eha, we're about to go fight, but Addison is on the other warship, so he managed to convince them to send help."

"Captain, this is the Fusilier," Wybert came over a separate channel. "My team has taken command of the Star Spear and four of the turrets directly. Can someone else handle the aft pair?"

"I'll handle it!" Aileen yelled. "Wybert, you face forward. I've got your spinnerets."

"Thank you, Commander," the Ilount said.

Lazarus studied the situation.

Dutra was deeper in the gravity well, with the ScoutWall above him if he tried to climb out to fight. Or he could run sideways, putting them on his tail and pointing his heavier guns the wrong direction.

Lazarus really needed to build a ship that could fight facing either direction, just like those old battleships that maritime navies had built to float on oceans. But wishes were fishes today.

"Fusilier, I have identified the vessel in command of the ScoutWall on your targeting systems," Lazarus said. "He is your primary target, as the senior officer will be there. The others will only have a Commander in charge. Remember that we are not as durable as they are, and the two escape pods have been lost, so everyone get into whatever life suits you can find right now and be prepared to abandon ship the hard way if we have to."

It would be one hell of an order, telling civilians to prepare to be sucked out a breach and into deep space, where they could hope that *Dutra* would be able to pick them up after the battle. Assuming the Rio Alliance won.

Some of them might be better off going down with the ship, rather than falling into Westphalian hands.

Lazarus took a deep breath and contemplated what he was about to order. How amazingly stupid it was.

And how right.

"Nav, accelerate to engage the enemy squadron," he ordered calmly.

FORTY-ONE

ADDISON

ADDISON HAD COILED off to one side, content to let the others handle this. All of them had many more years in uniform than he did, even the lowly lieutenant next to him had gone to a military university and gotten a degree.

Addison Wolcott had worked on the docks before finding a berth as a cargo punk, slowly working his way up to owning his own ship with a crew.

"Wolcott, what's the capability of that ship?" Carlos barked now. "And what is it, anyway?"

"*Astral Jewel* appears to be a small Security Barc, camouflaged as a private yacht," he replied.

He leaned over and touched the sensors officer's screen to mark several place on the exterior where it looked like things had been added or removed to change the silhouette of the ship. "Changes in these places that appear cosmetic. Main gun here. Several turrets here, here, and here."

"So that's an Innruld ship?" the woman turned to him.

Lieutenant Marie Oslor. He'd finally spent enough time around her to deal with her as a person. Too many of the others were just faces, but this many Humans in such a confined space tended to overwhelm him at times.

"What the Innruld might consider a warship," he corrected her. "Small one, compared to the big ones, but armed far heavier than most ships you will encounter."

"Captain, they're about to commit suicide," she called back over a shoulder. "Shields are like tissue paper and not nearly enough power signature to reinforce them against even a ScoutWall."

Addison felt his heart sink. Eha was aboard that ship, according to the hail they had sent back. Lazarus and the rest of the folks that had left on *Ajax*. And they were about to die.

Carlos looked his direction and scowled.

"Then we need to do something about that, folks," he snapped loudly. "Accelerate at them and prepare to get all their attention on us. Remember people, these are GunWall class ships, even if they've been modified for long-sailing. Big guns point forward and only the Powerbolt Cannons on the rims can shoot backwards. If that's all they have to engage *Astral Jewel*, maybe it will be enough."

"Captain?" Admiral da Silva started to say, but Carlos held up a finger to stop him.

"Rod, the Species Underground needs us to overthrow the Innruld," Carlos said, shifting to point at the screen at the front of the room. "That's them, right there. That ship needs to survive this battle more than *Dutra* does, because if we win, we can transfer everyone over to *Ajax* and plant my old ship right there instead. But that's Lazarus and the Ambassador. They are the war."

Rodrigo da Silva studied Carlos for a long moment, then turned to look at Addison.

"Understood, Captain," he said in a quieter voice. "Give 'em hell."

"That's the plan, sir," Carlos said. His voice rose. "Slow ahead, all generators to redline and everything we can spare into shields and guns, people. We need them pointing at us and not *Astral Jewel*. Fusilier, any ship that turns to engage Lazarus I want you to punish him for it with whatever Star Lance has bearing. Am I clear?"

"Affirmative, Captain!" someone yelled.

Addison hadn't spent nearly as much time with the fighting crew as the surveyors, but the man speaking had the same growl of confidence that Lazarus got in those moments. Must be a Rio Alliance Navy thing, but Addison would need that today.

"Carlos," Addison said in a quiet enough voice that the Gnashiiley could ignore him if he chose, but the Captain looked over expectantly.

"At Vilga's Stand, we got close to them to get their attention, and then backed away just fast enough to entice them, like galumphs outrunning hounds," Addison said.

"Backed away?" Carlos and da Silva said in harmony.

"Your engines are not producing thrust against physical space, unlike the more primitive ones on *Astral Jewel*," Addison reminded them. "They'll work just as well in reverse."

Carlos blinked several times. A light appeared in his eyes.

Addison had seen the same thing with Lazarus. They were trained to go right at a problem, with the big guns all facing forward because Humans had shoulders that could swing a club or sword with one hand while they carried a heavy shield with the other.

Churquen weren't built that way, so they had to get sideways to someone and whip the tail around them for a hard squeeze.

"Nav, bring me down and right a shade," Carlos ordered. "Maintain speed, but be prepared to slam everything backwards on my order to decelerate us to zero relative and then slither backwards away from those bastards. Fusilier, acknowledge movement orders and prepare accordingly."

"Got it, sir," the man over there said in a hungry voice.

Addison smiled grimly. Humans were going to invoke a revolution on Innruld Space. The Liberation that Lazarus had promised, but it looked like Addison Wolcott knew a few tricks that he could teach the Humans over there.

A GunWall was used to maneuvering sideways. The design hinged in the middle, so that the engines could rotate forward one hundred and ten degrees while keeping the gun shield and main armament pointed at a target. Just like a Churquen that way.

They should envision *Dutra* backing straight away from them in the manner of hungry fish going after an injured whale.

Dutra opened fire with the forward left Star Lance. The range was extreme, but Addison understood that the point wasn't to do damage so much as draw all attention this way.

So that *Astral Jewel*, and his love, might survive.

FORTY-TWO

LAZARUS

LAZARUS STUDIED THE SITUATION. This ship had come out of the graving dock with something like a heavy Powerbolt as the main armament, because this class of ship barely had the power for it. Singh and her people had fixed that, and then tuned all the existing generators and added new ones from stores.

He had power to spare. The problem was that he was flying in an eggshell.

"Fusilier, hold fire with the Star Lance for now," he ordered. "All turrets stand by to engage with target number three."

All of the ScoutWall ships were moving to engage *Dutra*, even as the big ship charged forward to fight them. Lazarus was reminded of the ancient bull fighting, where acrobats would tumble over the horns of a charging bull unharmed, perhaps plucking a scarf as they went by as a way of measuring their skill.

The Phalanx variants were maneuvering outwards now to surround the bull, while *Astral Jewel* was still too far away to do much of anything. The Star Lance could reach, but he wanted that as a surprise.

"Kuei, move us closer," Lazarus ordered. "Other turrets, open fire at extreme range."

It was about as dangerous as tickling someone, to hit them with Innruld Powerbolts from this range. And if one of them came over there, Lazarus was pretty sure they would stomp on this Innruld Security Barc like a bug.

But the Rio Alliance had come to their senses. Had listened and sent help. He just needed to make sure that Westphalia couldn't exploit this knowledge. Short term, the Humans of Earth would be happy blowing up Innruld ships and stations to assert their authority, which would help, but Lazarus needed to keep them on the far side of the nebula as long as possible.

All six turrets opened fire. The effect was probably comparable to walking in the rain without a hat, but he wanted them miserable and hunched over, even as *Dutra* opened fire with her two big guns and Westphalia answered with their Star Lances.

At least Wybert understood tactical use of big guns now, having used Kirov's Lance to such amazing effect at Vilga's Stand.

"*Hey, that's weird,*" Cormac suddenly piped up.

It was never going to be a good thing when an electronic lifeform found something *weird*.

"Talk to me," Lazarus called to the NavCrawler.

"Dutra *has begun slowing down,*" Cormac said. "*Engine signatures suggest the ship is going to come to a complete halt in front of the closing ScoutWall. Lazarus, why would Captain Nguema make such a tactical mistake?*"

Lazarus didn't know Carlos Nguema by name. But the Patrol wing of the fleet and the experimental wing where he had worked rarely crossed paths. He did know Admiral da Silva. And Addison was on that ship, so they should be asking the man the same question.

Addison. Of course.

"Kuei, he's about to go retrograde on them," Lazarus laughed. "Just like we did at Vilga. Addison must have explained it to him."

"Think they'll actually fall for it?" she looked back over a shoulder.

"They did then," he countered. "I would have, until Addison taught me something I'd never considered doing."

"How does that change our shooting priorities?" Wybert came over the intercom.

Lazarus stopped and considered the situation. Yup, Wybert was growing up and acting like a proper officer. But then, he'd come of age at Vilga's Stand.

Ajax was down below them in the gravity well. *Dutra* above that, but she'd be backing away shortly and probably maintaining relative elevation above the blue ice giant. The ScoutWall above and trailing, but chasing after him, as long as Lazarus didn't give them a reason to turn back immediately.

"All turrets, reduce your rate of fire fifty percent," Lazarus called. "Pretend like we're the same underpowered slug you had before, and the idiot captain has just diverted power to the engines. Kuei, flare us off a flank a little so that we're not right behind them, but maybe somebody could take the occasional potshot at us over their shoulder or with that rear Powerbolt they have above the engines. Distraction, but not threat. Not yet. Fusilier, when we get to the edge of optimum for the Star Lance, divert all gunnery power to your station and let loose as fast as you can recharge your capacitors."

Acknowledgments all the way around.

Lazarus smiled grimly at Aileen, watched her return it with a nod.

"Charge."

FORTY-THREE

ADDISON

ADDISON STUDIED the screen over Marie's shoulder, but it seemed to be working. *Dutra* had come to rest in orbit, relative to the closing ships, and was now backing away like a stoned Churquen on ice. The air between them fluoresced regularly as bolts ionized the thin atmosphere at this altitude, until it was almost like trying to land on a planetary surface in a lightning storm.

Star Lances were powerful beams, but *Dutra* only had two. Three of the four Star Spears on the corners of the ship could also engage, with four Star Spears and a single Star Lance coming back at them from the ScoutWall. *Dutra* had power for shields. The Phalanx variants all had that gun shield itself when shots penetrated the force shielding. Powerbolts went back and forth like angry woodpeckers.

"Did they do this at Vilga, Addison?" Carlos called as the ship fell into a rhythm.

"Similar, yes," Addison replied. "Wybert was sniping away with Kirov's Lance, and a square hit from that could punch through damaged shields and make it through the gun shield as well. But we'd also dropped out right on top of them, blown up a Heavy Starcruiser, and then goaded them into chasing us. They weren't thinking all that straight."

"Good thing I've got your slithery tracks to follow then, isn't it?" Carlos grinned.

Addison chuckled. Gnashiiley. From intimating creatures to goofballs comparable to Wybert on a silly day.

What was the galaxy coming to?

The entire hull rocked now and the bridge went dark for a long second before secondary systems kicked in.

"What was that?" Carlos called to the room.

"Front shields are pretty much down, sir," someone replied. "Regenerating now, but it is going to take some time."

"Roger that," Carlos said. He looked at Addison for a moment and that light came on in his eyes again. "Nav, begin a spiraling motion as part of our reverse. Gimme a slither on the bow so they can pound on the forward flank shields for a while. Damage Control teams, we'll need all guns soon, so prioritize those."

Addison listened to the acknowledgments roll in. The crew was loose. Even joking with each other. He hoped that was a good sign. They had damaged two of the Phalanx Scouts pretty well, but suffered a lot of abuse themselves.

However, as Carlos had said, a ScoutWall was probably a little bit too much for *Dutra* to handle on most days.

Hopefully, that wasn't going to be today.

"Captain, message from *Astral Jewel*," Marie suddenly spoke up. "Lazarus says stand by for a surprise."

"Addison?" Carlos asked.

"No clue," he replied. "But it's Lazarus talking."

"Noted," Carlos said. "Engineering, I need you to take all the generators to the edge and hold them, starting in ten seconds. Gunnery, assume that little pixie of a ship has a surprise and the ScoutWall is about to flinch hard before they catch themselves."

"Roger that."

Addison held his breath as he found himself leaning almost on Marie's shoulder to watch what she was seeing.

Dutra, backing away and starting to roll inside a log. Five stalkers giving chase, two injured and two relatively unharmed, plus the CommandScout that was sitting back and sniping. *Astral Jewel*, sitting up on a high corner, almost like a hawk.

"Sir?" Marie asked.

Addison realized he was muttering in her ear.

"Carlos," he turned. "Think hawk."

The Gnashiiley studied his screens for a moment.

"Yes," he agreed. "Gunnery, I want everything on the command ship over there when you let loose. Ignore the rest for now."

Addison nodded. He was even beginning to think like a Rio Alliance naval officer, scary as that might be.

Warrior, when all he had wanted was to make a living and maybe live free.

But those bastards were threatening Eha and Lazarus and everyone else.

That would not stand.

FORTY-FOUR

LAZARUS

"KUEI, NOW!" Lazarus yelled, maybe a little louder than necessary, but they'd been trailing the enemy squadron for too long, pecking away with those teeny things that the Innruld might have deluded themselves into calling Powerbolts. "Wybert, whenever you're ready."

Dutra was hurt. Maybe bad. He'd gone into a maneuver Lazarus could only compare to a gator rolling. Or maybe someone had drawn inspiration from a Churquen?

Lazarus grinned.

Admiral Santos was never going to rid the fleet of an infection of new ideas, was he?

Astral Jewel's bow suddenly slewed around like a hog on ice. They'd still be sliding forward for a while, but now the whole ship was pointed inwards, diving into the gravity well of the ice giant and aiming for a lower orbit than the one they'd maintained for so long.

One that just happening to cut right across the stern of the enemy squadron at short range.

The lights flickered as Wybert finally got to act, blasting away with the Star Spear in the overhead turret. His target was the command vessel, on the logic that any of the ships might manage to escape and make it home, but the best records would be aboard that ship.

Lazarus smiled as he realized that they had lulled Westphalia to sleep. The first shot took the CommandWall in a flank without any reinforcements on the shielding. That barrier went down and some of the energy got through, flashing a small plume of debris from the hull metal just behind the engine hinge.

Then the second bolt slammed home.

Physics was physics. The energy caused a detonation directly on the skin and interior chambers of the vessel. That turned into a geyser of pressurized atmosphere bleeding out, and a cloud of superheated plasma as well. Something must have broken inside, because instead of adjusting, the whole ship pivoted on its nose instead of the hinge like Wybert had just hit it with a baseball bat.

A moment later, *Dutra* spoke up, with one Star Lance slamming into the forward shielding and the shield itself, but the second getting past as the CommandWall ship rotated on a flat plane.

The hinge broke.

Lazarus had never seen that happen, in all the battles he'd been in or studied. There were lots of ways for a ship to suffer a catastrophic failure, especially a GunWall ship. The hinge was not supposed to break like that. The fore and aft halves of the ship began moving in different directions.

Lazarus started to order Wybert after another target, but the Ilount had already moved on, shifting his beam to the nearest Phalanx as that ship began to madly pivot himself to bring the shield around to protect himself against *Astral Jewel*. Something. Anything.

All six turrets opened up as well now, so presumably the Fusilier had ordered it. Even Aileen was getting into the action. Rain, but maybe it was starting to freeze into hail at this range and hurt.

Certainly, the enemy squadron began to panic.

Lazarus checked his screens and realized that *Dutra* was slowing down again, like he was about to stop and give chase.

Four little birdies flushed by a hunting dog.

Three. Wybert got a bolt home on one of the damaged ones and that ship started to tumble.

Dutra picked on the only really undamaged one left, hitting the ship suddenly with everything that Patrol Cruiser had. Six local turrets piled in as well. Pieces started coming off.

Flanked was a horrible way to find yourself in a fracas like this.

Wybert moved on. *Dutra* moved on. Incoming fire was starting to hurt as the front shield tore to ribbons, but nobody over there had a Star Spear that they could point at *Astral Jewel* without letting *Dutra* come up behind them with a knife.

"*Sir, we're being hailed by a Westphalian vessel,*" Cormac suddenly broke in. "*What does it mean* Asking for terms?"

Lazarus studied the message readout. Blinked in surprise, and then reached out and cut the guns off from firing.

"Cormac, tell *Dutra* to hold fire as well," Lazarus ordered with a grim smile. "They are asking to surrender to us."

FORTY-FIVE
ADDISON

ADDISON WATCHED the badly mauled Westphalian squadron maneuver as best they could. Their leader had actually broken into two pieces, both of which were deorbiting fast enough that they would fall into the planet below in a few days. Two others could barely limp into position to be covered by friendly guns. That left two ships, one that had been in reasonably good shape after they reset a number of breakers and one that might manage to limp home in a month, if they were lucky.

"Well, Commander?" Admiral da Silva asked with a broad smile on his face as they both looked around *Dutra's* bridge and noted the cleanup getting close to finishing. "What do you think?"

"This was my third battle," Addison replied evenly. "The pirates were no threat to *Ajax*. Vilga's Stand was more even. It and today rank high in unbelievable carnage. What will you do with all these sailors?"

"Even in war, there are rules, Addison," da Silva replied. "They have honorably surrendered to us, so for now we will put two officers each aboard their vessels to take command."

"And they will just follow a Rio Alliance officer?" Addison was surprised. "Just like that?"

"Obviously, the folks we would send would be Humans," da Silva nodded, indicating Addison and Carlos with a gesture. "No reason to put temptation in front of anyone."

"Just like that?" Addison pressed.

"Yes," Rodrigo turned serious. "Carlos's and his people will escort them to the nearest Rio port, where the vessels would normally be interred and maybe traded home at some point, along with the crews, but these might be too broken to be worth it."

"What about Yisan?" Addison queried.

"What about it?"

"If they are honorable about such things, as strange as that is to imagine, could you have them go to Yisan and turn themselves over to the local authorities?" Addison asked. "Would they take that deal? Perhaps leave their ships and trade them for passage home on a Westphalian hull?"

"What on earth for, Addison?" da Silva asked, his voice coming up a little.

Addison gestured for Carlos to come close as he looked up at the sound.

"What's up?" Carlos asked as he stepped close.

"I was asking if your officers could sail the surviving vessels to Yisan without *Dutra* babysitting them," Addison explained.

"Why?"

"I need you here, Carlos," Addison said bluntly. "*Dutra*. We've got *Ajax* and *Astral Jewel*, but not that many Humans or Moah or Gnashiiley like you, to say nothing of Atomarsk like H'Brige Slani. The whole point of this mission was to go to Innruld Space and do something. If you have to return to Rio for repairs and escort duty, it will be how long before another ship can come?"

"I'll send someone as fast as I can convince Pedro," da Silva spoke up.

"That's my point," Addison pressed. "Convince people. Do something. Bureaucratic inertia. Vilga's Stand would have fallen, because nobody can move quickly. Plus, you've got lots of spare engineers that could take command of Westphalian ships for now. Lazarus tells me that looks good on a resume later, assuming all goes well."

"But Yisan?" da Silva circled back to that point.

"Salvage," Addison said. "Those hulls have to be worth a lot of money, even as badly damaged as they are. Let the Westphalian ships in harbor haul the crews home, and let the wealthy oligarchs of Yisan show a profit from helping you. That will make them happier, and it really is the biggest star port with repair and salvage facilities between here and anywhere."

"I will consider it," da Silva announced. "After we talk to Lazarus and to Eha Dunham, however. Carlos, operations will continue as normal for now."

For now.

Addison latched onto that point and hoped. Even damaged, *Dutra* was more than a match for almost anything it would encounter in Innruld Space.

He could not let the chance to break the Innruld for good slither past him.

Hopefully, Eha could convince the man.

FORTY-SIX

LAZARUS

LAZARUS STUDIED the situation on his screens as the pincke bringing the admiral and the others over to *Ajax* approached the dock aft. He'd left Cormac, Singh, and Afolayan aboard *Astral Jewel* with most of her engineers to repair things. It would make a lovely, sneaky surprise one of these days.

Wybert sat next to Kuei on the much-larger bridge and had all the guns ready to fire, even as the ship itself was still warming up from the cold storage they had left it in before.

Aileen was on his left and Eha on his right, with Grace and Alla beyond that.

"It's time," Aileen said.

He trusted her sense of time and rose immediately.

"H'Brige, could you meet us in the conference room aft?" he called over the line back to engineering as he joined the women headed towards the hatch.

The bridge was forward and the landing bay was aft, but he had the slidewalk. It had taken Eha some time to understand the physics, but she and Alla moved rapidly now, pushing off like sidewinders and threatening to leave him behind.

Lucas escorted the admiral into the room a few minutes after they arrived, with a Gnashiiley, presumably Captain Nguema, as well as High Councilor Teixeira, and Addison.

Wolcott came to a dead stop in the doorway as he looked at Eha, his eyeslits opening about as far as Lazarus had ever seen them move. Addison even sputtered for a moment.

"You never told me," he whispered in an accusational tone, staring at Eha.

Lazarus looked at the woman in time to see all of her scales flare up in embarrassment and her eyeslits pinch almost shut.

"How long?" Addison demanded quietly, seemingly unaware that every person in the room was staring at him now.

"Three more months," Eha whispered.

Then she grinned so big Lazarus thought it might hurt.

Addison collapsed onto his coil and just sat there for a moment.

"Could someone please explain?" Admiral da Silva asked in a loud, impersonal tone, even as he was staring directly at Lazarus. "Interlac or Portuguese? Either works for me."

"Good news, Admiral da Silva," Alla spoke up, drawing all eyes to her now.

"And you would be?" da Silva asked dryly, turning his whole body to face her.

"Alla Dunham," she said. "Eha's mother."

"Madam," he bowed. "And the good news?"

"I'm about to be a grandmother," Alla beamed.

Lazarus smiled. From the gasps, exclamations, and cheers around the room, nobody had known but the two Churquen women. Even he had only guessed, but Eha had asked him to keep it secret.

Of course, how does one identify pregnancy in an alien species?

"Congratulations," Councilor Teixeira smiled as she sat. "Could everyone join me, please?"

She got everyone settled. Introductions went quickly. Lazarus felt some of the mad energy bleed out of the room. Or maybe get absorbed by the Councilor. That woman had a predatory smile.

"I am here as a representative of the High Council and the government itself," she announced for the ones who had never met her before. "Admiral da Silva represents the fleet. Madams Dunham, I presume the two of you will speak for the Species Underground?"

"That is correct," Eha replied.

To Lazarus, it was obvious that the two women had sparred before, but both seemed to respect each other. And it was a good sign that the government had sent her on what amounted to a fact-finding mission into hostile territory.

"There is a discussion about sending the captured ships to a neutral port as a way of keeping *Dutra* on station," Teixeira began. "Personally, I'm in favor of that because my mission needs to continue into Innruld Space, but I would also understand if we did end up having to transfer to *Ajax* for that. However, I've also just arrived on the scene, and you are flying what appears to be a stolen Security Barc, according to Commander Wolcott. What other surprises should be I be preparing myself for?"

Lazarus had already studied the newcomers. Rodrigo he knew pretty well as a commanding officer. Teixeira he had heard about from both Eha and Grace. Nguema was a stranger, but being Gnashiiley would change the man's approach to many things when dealing with the Innruld.

However, he felt his eyes drawn to Eha, even before she took the kind of breath that automatically got your attention.

Time for the other shoe to drop.

"Madam Dunham?" Teixeira asked.

"As part of a small raid on Gowook, we were able to break Innruld control of a significant amount of the planet, at least for a few days, perhaps as much as two weeks," Eha began, even as Addison let out a strangled squawk of surprise. "At that moment, as many ships as were able to were planning to lift from the surface with as much of the local Underground infrastructure as possible, to rendezvous at a previously selected location."

"To what end?" Teixeira asked in the sort of tone that reminded you she'd been a lawyer at some point.

"Their goal was to flee into the darkness, away from Innruld control," Eha said. "With local flight control destroyed and the hall of records burned, they stand a good chance of making it to a world where they could set up a new colony. One free of the Innruld."

Teixeira waited with a polite smile on her face, like she could smell that shoe getting ready to land somewhere close.

"Originally, my hope was to present the Rio Alliance with a *fait accompli*," Eha continued. "But since you're here, I need to ask for your permission and hope for the best."

"Where were you thinking of resettling your refugees, Eha?" the woman asked.

Lazarus felt his breath catch as he waited. Everyone in here was on pins and needles.

"6357 Wei Xiu," Eha replied simply. "Vilga's Stand."

Teixeira waited for a long beat, studying everyone on this side of the table before she spoke.

"How many people are we talking?" she finally asked, which was far better than an immediate rejection.

"We won't know until we rendezvous with them," Alla spoke up now. "Median calculations suggest around three thousand Churquen and up to two thousand other species, heavy on Moah and Yithadreph, based on the population statistics of Ersop and the Underground membership."

"Five thousand?" Teixeira asked. "What's your best top-end estimate?"

"Ten, if everyone manages, nothing goes wrong, and the Innruld are completely flatfooted by the whole situation, which they might be."

"How much land would you expect to claim, given an entire planet?" Teixeira pressed, getting legalistic now with her tone.

"Not that much," Alla said. "A city ten miles on a side, plus sufficient farmland that we can start growing crops. Hopefully, the Rio Alliance would open the world up sooner than expected and we could have neighbors. We will be starting from zero to build an industrial base, and we need your technology anyway, as everything we do is several generations behind Humans, according to Lazarus."

He felt the Councilor's eyes zero in on him, and then she turned to look at Addison, who might have finally recovered.

"I am not empowered by the Council to make those sorts of decisions," she said.

Everyone slumped in defeat.

"However," she continued before anyone could speak, "the High Council recently found it necessary to deal with an unregistered colony on 9087 Geminorum IV and we established a precedent that those miners could have the territory they had claimed on the day a certain Rio Alliance warship rescued them from pirates."

She beamed at them now.

"I believe we can find a way to set you down and make it successful enough, ladies," she said to Eha and Alla. "After all, isn't the entire point of the Rio Alliance making sure that all the species in the galaxy come together as equals and friends?"

This time the cheers were even louder, and Lazarus found himself among those making the most noise.

Maybe, just maybe he could help his new friends escape.

FORTY-SEVEN

ADDISON

ADDISON HAD RETIRED to his and Eha's rooms. He held her as tightly as his coil would allow. She kissed his cheeks and his brow. Both of them were crying.

"We've done it," he finally managed to whisper.

"We have," she laughed quietly. "Who would have imagined?"

"All those years were not wasted," he reminded her. "Good things are coming out of them."

He untangled himself enough to study her. Not many people would realize the truth, but Churquen would. And if she still had a few months, then this might be the first birth on a new world.

A new tomorrow.

He smiled at the thought, and then flinched.

"What is it, my love?" Eha asked.

"I can't go with you," he said, looking up to see the pain take root in her eyes.

"Surely, you've done enough," Eha cried.

"You must go to Vilga," he countered. "The colony will need you. But Lazarus will need me here in Innruld Space."

She wanted to argue with him. Yell, rant, something. He could see it in her eyes and feel it in her tail.

At the same time, she knew the truth. The war had only begun. One small colony of Churquen would not be enough. They would need to free the others. While keeping the specists of Westphalia from reaching Innruld Space.

At least the Rio Alliance had hopefully chosen to live up to their founding documents. The statement of all sentients everywhere being born equal.

> *"Quando no curso de eventos*
> *Humanos…"*
> *"When in the course of Human*
> *events…"*

"You're right," she said, lapsing into a defeat so badly that he just held her close.

"The Species Underground cannot do much to help," he said. "Not today. They will provide an inspiration for the Humans, though. Just as the Humans will inspire us to finally rise up. But I must be at Dormell. At Zhoonarrim. Even Gowook."

"What about Alla?" Eha asked. "She could take your place."

"Not with Carlos and Admiral da Silva," Addison countered, holding her close and rocking her. "Nor with Teixeira. She is a stranger to them, and I might have become a friend. She will go with you and you two will set up the colony. I will come later, after we have done our job."

He smothered her tears with kisses for now. All too soon, they would be parted again, but good things would come of it this time.

And he had her tonight.

FORTY-EIGHT

LAZARUS

LAZARUS STUDIED THE ADMIRAL. This was a military meeting, such as it might be, so all the civilians had been politely excluded. It was him, da Silva, Nguema, and Addison. Weird, but necessary.

"This meeting will come to order," da Silva began. "Admiral Rodrigo da Silva commanding."

He paused now to study the three of them.

"Excluding the three captured vessels that will be departing shortly, I have three warships in various states of readiness. *Dutra* can be repaired reasonably well with available crew and supplies, even after pulling crew members for the reflagged vessels. *Astral Jewel* suffered no lasting damage. *Ajax* is fully operational."

Lazarus watched Rodrigo chew on his next words for a moment while everyone watched.

"In any other circumstances, I would send *Astral Jewel* to Vilga's Stand," he finally began. "It is the least combat-worthy vessel and perfect as an escort. However, I need it here as a scout. Commander Wolcott, you will take command of *Astral Jewel*. We will work out your crew requirements shortly."

"Understood, sir," Addison replied quietly.

Lazarus felt his pain. That was one of the reasons why he'd never married, those long voyages away from your spouse, coming home frequently to a stranger you shared your bed with and kids that didn't know you. It had happened to too many of his friends.

"Captain Nguema, normally I would keep you on station with me," da Silva continued. "I hope you will not take this as a personal affront, but I need you to deliver the colonists to Vilga's Stand, lay in any supplies you can bribe or wheedle out of whoever is in command of the station overhead, and then race back here as rapidly as you can."

Lazarus watched the man brighten from his slump. Even his tail feathers stood up straight.

"My pilot, Kuei Akeley, has a route mapped, Captain," Lazarus said. "Akeley's Passage. It will get you back from Vilga and through to Dormell rapidly, and we'll leave you coordinates and a beacon on the far side, since it's no longer safe to leave a ship in this system."

Smiles around the table. Westphalia likely wouldn't have been able to find *Ajax*, without knowing exactly where to look, but they would return here eventually.

That was when the trouble would start, as they slowly found the hidden paths to the other side of the nebula and Innruld Space.

"Captain Oliveira," da Silva began, looking squarely at him now. "*Pancho. Lazarus.* Councilor Teixeira is going to accompany the colonists and then either return home or catch a ride with *Dutra*, which puts me out at the tip of the spear. The politicians at Brasilia will be measuring our actions with the exacting science of hindsight. Am I clear?"

"I am exquisitely familiar with the feeling, sir," he smiled.

"Yes, I suppose you would be," da Silva noted dryly. "You will take command of *Ajax* and work with Commander Wolcott to scout enemy territory. After touring *Astral Jewel*, I am reasonably confident that you can allow any Innruld warship to fire the first salvo at *Ajax*, thereby provoking us while not putting my valuable carcass at risk."

Everyone snickered at that, including the admiral. Lazarus nodded.

"Your thoughts, Lazarus?" he asked.

"In my mind and my logs, I have called this a war of liberation, Admiral," Lazarus said. "I have liberally quoted the Charter of the Rio Alliance itself, both there and with folks like Addison and Eha.

> *Quando no curso de eventos*
> *Humanos…*
> *When in the course of Human events…*

It will not be enough to simply liberate the Species from the Innruld, sir. We will have to keep Westphalia at bay while we do, and then use the strength and help of our new friends to keep Earth itself at bay."

"You're gambling a lot with this, Lazarus," da Silva said sternly.

"Yes, sir," Lazarus agreed. "However, it is the right thing to do."

READ MORE

Be sure to read all the books in the Lazarus Alliance series!

Escape
Return
Rebellion
Revolution
Liberation
Retribution
Alliance

Available at your favorite retailers!

ABOUT THE AUTHOR

Blaze Ward writes science fiction in the Alexandria Station universe (Jessica Keller, The Science Officer, The Story Road, etc.) as well as several other science fiction universes, such as Star Dragon, the Dominion, and more. He also writes odd bits of high fantasy with swords and orcs. In addition, he is the Editor and Publisher of *Boundary Shock Quarterly Magazine*. You can find out more at his website www.blazeward.com, as well as Facebook, Goodreads, and other places.

Blaze's works are available as ebooks, paper, and audio, and can be found at a variety of online vendors. His newsletter comes out regularly, and you can also follow his blog on his website. He really enjoys interacting with fans, and looks forward to any and all questions—even ones about his books!

Never miss a release!

If you'd like to be notified of new releases, sign up for my newsletter.

http://www.blazeward.com/newsletter/

Buy More!

Did you know that you can buy directly from my website?

https://www.blazeward.com/shop/

Connect with Blaze!

Web: www.blazeward.com
Boundary Shock Quarterly (BSQ):
https://www.boundaryshockquarterly.com/

ABOUT KNOTTED ROAD PRESS

Knotted Road Press fiction specializes in dynamic writing set in mysterious, exotic locations.

Knotted Road Press non–fiction publishes autobiographies, business books, cookbooks, and how–to books with unique voices.

Knotted Road Press creates DRM–free ebooks as well as high–quality print books for readers around the world.

With authors in a variety of genres including literary, poetry, mystery, fantasy, and science fiction, Knotted Road Press has something for everyone.

Knotted Road Press
www.KnottedRoadPress.com

Revolution
The Lazarus Alliance: Book Four
Blaze Ward
Copyright © 2021 Blaze Ward
All rights reserved
Published by Knotted Road Press
www.KnottedRoadPress.com

ISBN: 978-1-64470-200-0

Cover art:

ID 76082241 © Luca Oleastri | Dreamstime.com

Cover and interior design copyright © 2021 Knotted Road Press

Reviews
It's true. Reviews help. Even a short one, such as, "Loved it!" So please consider reviewing this book (and all of the ones you've read) on your favorite retailer site.

Never miss a release!
If you'd like to be notified of new releases, sign up for my newsletter.

http://www.blazeward.com/newsletter/

Buy More!
Did you know that you can buy directly from my website?

https://www.blazeward.com/shop/